D0777954

Ain't No Secret Safe in the Dark

Sharmeka Ballard

KN
AUG 17

Printed in the United States of America
First Printing, 2016

ISBN: 978-1-5356-0702-5

Dedication

This book is dedicated to all the men and women who can relate to this.

Acknowledgments

First and foremost, I would like to thank GOD. Without Him, none of this would be possible. I am blessed by Him each and every day. It was the strength from GOD that allowed me to put this together.

I would also like to thank all my family, friends, co-workers, and everyone who has been there for me. There are too many of you to name, but I appreciate you all and all of your support.

Contents

Chapter One

"So THIS IS WHAT LIFE is all about—growing up, finishing school, getting married, having kids, and now getting a fucking divorce!" Joy yelled as she headed downstairs to her kitchen to get something to drink. She had been in bed half the day after she took her daughter to school. She had taken the day off so she could try to clear her head. She was in the middle of a nasty divorce with her husband of seven years. He had cheated on her and had a baby with the bitch. This wasn't the first time he had fucked around on her, but it was the first time he had gotten another bitch pregnant, so Joy wanted to divorce his ass. What really had her pissed was the fact that he was trying to get full custody of their daughter Cherish. Cherish was four going on five, and she was a smart little something. Joy loved her daughter with all her heart; she was her miracle child. See, doctors had told Joy that she would never be able to have kids, so she and Paul were thinking of adopting. Then one day out of the blue, she felt sick and noticed that her period hadn't come in a month. She really didn't think much of it, being that her periods were so irregular anyways, but she ended up going to the doctor, and that's when he gave her the best news of her life.

"Joy, I don't know how to tell you this," the doctor said to her. Joy's heart was pounding so fast, and she was so nervous. She thought that something was really wrong with her. She was terrified and wished like hell her husband could be there to comfort her. "This is truly amazing, seeing how the odds were against you, but you are four weeks pregnant!" Dr. Cho said with a huge smile on his face. The way he looked, you would think that he was the father. Joy was sitting in a state of shock, and her body was numb. She let out a long sigh of relief and began to cry tears of joy. She couldn't wait to tell Paul, so she pulled out her phone without even saying anything to the doctor.

"Babe, you won't believe this! Oh my God, baby, you won't freaking believe this shit. God is really truly the best. I am four weeks pregnant!" Joy told him in an excited tone.

Paul was so happy that he began to scream, and people around him looked at him like he was crazy. "Oh shit, I'm having a baby! Oh shit, we're having a fucking baby! I can't believe it. I told you, baby, those doctors didn't know what they were talking about. We're having a baby! I'm about to leave work and come home to my baby momma, so we can celebrate. I love you, baby!" Paul said as he was smiling. He was so happy, and Joy was even happier. She hung the phone after telling him she loved him, too. Joy finished up with the doctor then headed home.

Nine months and thirteen hours of labor later, baby Cherish Miracle Carter was born. Joy had loved and cherished her daughter since the day she brought her home, so there was no way in hell she was going to let Paul take her child away from her.

Back then, they were so in love, and things between them were great, so Joy couldn't understand what made him want to go out and fuck around. Then again, that is the million-dollar question every woman in the world wants to know. Paul and Joy met at a strip club one night when she was out with her girl Keyshia celebrating her birthday. Joy and Keyshia's hot asses were up in the club living it up. This was one club that everybody and their momma was up in, even though it was so damn small. That shit was jumping all the time. Most females acted all stank about going to a strip club, but that shit there was all the way live all the time. Keyshia and Joy were in there almost every weekend, like they were two of the strippers. Their other home girl wasn't really into it that much. Being that they were regulars, even at their tender age, everyone knew them in there, and they knew most of the all the real niggas. So Joy was real curious when she saw this fine-ass dark-skinned, clean-shaven, medium-built, Morris Chestnut-looking nigga standing by the bar. To her that nigga was so damn fine that just looking at him got her pussy moist. The nigga was all that and more; you would have thought he was a celebrity or something. Joy was all into his swag. He didn't act like most of the niggas in there. He was laid-back, chilling, and vibing to the music, dressed in all Polo with a fresh cut and some pearly white teeth—aw man, she had to find out who this dude was! But one thing Joy was not was a groupie; her rule was never to sweat a nigga, no matter how much money he flashed in her face or how fine he was. She would make him chase her, but there was something about Paul that she couldn't shake. She had to have him.

Joy tapped Keyshia and whispered in her ear, "Damn, Kesh, I've never seen dude over there in the all-gray Polo before. I want him. Shit, I wanna give him this pussy." They both burst into laughter. Keyshia took a look for herself to see exactly who Joy was bragging about. Now, Keyshia was the opposite of Joy. She was much wilder than Joy was, being that she had grown up in a broken home. She felt that there was no one there for her, so she began to look for love and attention in the arms of any man who would show her affection. Joy always tried to keep Keyshia on her level and keep her out of trouble, but as long as she had known Keyshia, she had always done her thing. Joy never judged her friend. They'd been tight since elementary school, so she was there for her no matter what. She just hoped that one day she would get her shit together.

"Damn, you ain't lying! That motherfucker is fine. I will swallow all that nigga's babies."

"Bitch, you are so damn nasty, but shit, his ass is fine as hell. He can get this pussy right here in the club like Usher's song says."

They both started laughing. Joy then saw him look their way and smile. When he did that, she almost melted right there. "Oh shit! He saw us watching him. That is so embarrassing! I don't want this nigga to know we're over here sweating his ass."

"Ho, who is we? You're the one over here 'bout to catch a nut just by looking at this nigga. But maybe it's best you catch your nut like this cause we both know you ain't gon holla 'cause you ain't 'bout that life," Keyshia said to Joy and chuckled.

"What the fuck ever. I may not act all desperate, but I bet your ass before we leave this club, I'll get him!"

They always made bets like this, and Keyshia would always win, so she wasn't the least bit worried. She knew that Joy would let this nigga walk right out of here, and that would be some money in her pockets. "Okay, now here you go again. You're betting on something you ain't going to do. You're not sick of me taking your money by now? I'm just saying," Keyshia said to Joy with a smirk on her face.

"Shut the fuck up, bitch! Like I said, I will get that number tonight!" Joy told Keyshia with so much confidence in her voice. Then she took a sip of her Grey Goose and cranberry. Keyshia nodded her head to Joy, and then they began to vibe to the sounds of Billy Blue coming through the speakers. The club was packed, and they were having a blast. Joy was vibing so hard that she never even noticed Paul staring at her from the bar. He was fascinated by her long sexy legs, her pecan-tan skin complexion, slim waist, fat ass, and cute face. Joy was looking right that night in her catch-me, fuck-me black dress and red bottoms, and she had her hair long and wavy damn near to her ass. Paul wasn't paying attention to any of the bitches trying to give him a dance. He had one mission and one thing on his mind, and that was to get Joy. Paul was thinking, *Damn, li'l mama's fine as fuck.* He made a note to himself that he was going to get her number before he left that night. Paul never really rolled with a lot of dudes, but that night he was with his main man Slim. Every time they hit the club, Slim would blow all his money on the strippers, and Paul just vibed and let his boy do his thing. Slim got up and came to the bar to holla at his boy. "Damn, nigga, you good over here? I see how you're sweating shorty over there in the black dress. I must say she is a bad one. Shit, I will give her all my money, and she ain't even got to take off her clothes."

They both laughed and watched her as she bounced her ass to the beat of "Bounce that Ass Up and Down." Paul could feel his manhood jump each time she made her ass jump to the beat. "Man, Slim, I'mma make her mine. Hell yeah, I gotta have li'l mama. And she looks like she's independent, like she's running things. I would never think to wife nothing out of the club, but it's something 'bout shorty. I'm drawn to her. I've got to have her," Paul told Slim as he continued to stare at Joy.

"Say no more. Do your thang, bruh" Slim said. They slapped five with each other, and then Slim grabbed another chick to dance for him.

Paul called the bartender and asked her what Joy was drinking and said to take her whatever she and her friend was having. The bartender left, got the drinks, and headed over to Joy and Keyshia.

"Excuse me!" the bartender said to Joy. It was so loud that Joy could barely hear her, so she tapped her on the shoulder. "Hey, dude over there wanted me to give y'all these drinks," the bartender said, looking in Paul's direction to let Joy know who she was talking about.

Joy glanced across the room to see who she was referring to, and that's when she saw Paul standing there smiling at her. That really made her pussy jump, and she could feel her juices flow. She whispered something in the bartender's ear to tell him, gave her a tip, and then lifted her drink in Paul's direction, nodding to tell him thanks. Joy sipped on her drink and continued to dance to the music. Keyshia was all into the music, but she noticed the eye contact between Paul and Joy. The way they were looking at each other, you would have thought they were fucking. Keyshia was shocked at how her girl was really vibing to the music and just bouncing her ass all up and down. She was really putting on a show for Paul, and he was enjoying every moment of it. Joy was normally cool, and she would dance, but tonight she was on one. Keyshia thought to herself, *Damn, I'm about to lose this damn bet.* She let out a little chuckle to herself and continued sipping on her drink.

Paul couldn't take it anymore. He wanted Joy bad—real bad. Little did he know, she felt the same way. So he headed over to her, and she tried to act as if she hadn't seen him coming. She turned her back to his direction and began to dance, making her ass bounce up and down. Paul was damn near running over to her. He walked up behind her and whispered in her ear, "Damn, ma, you can't be doing this to a nigga."

The sweet smell of his Issey Miyake cologne and his sexy voice made her body tingle. "And what am I doing to you that is so wrong?" Joy whispered back in a flirtatious voice.

"You already know what you doing to me, ma! I can't even lie. You got a nigga sweating, so tell me, can I have you?"

"It depends on what way you want to have me," Joy responded.

"Umm, in all ways possible, baby. Damn, you're looking real good, and you smell delicious. Let a nigga get ya number, so we can chill sometimes."

Joy normally hated when a nigga talked about "Let's chill sometimes." That shit was such a turn-off for her. But for some reason, Paul made her body melt, and she wanted to feel his body all over hers. She turned to face him all the way and noticed the bulge in his pants. All she could think was, *Damn, and this nigga packing. Oh, hell yeah.*

They exchanged numbers. He called her that next day, and they hit it off from there. They dated a while, and then he felt she was the one for him. They were so in love, and they both felt they had found their soulmate. There was negative talk and negative feedback about their relationship, but they didn't let that stop them from being together. Now look: Seven years and one child later, they're getting a divorce. Joy slammed the fridge as the thoughts ran through her head. She really couldn't believe what was going on in her life. She was a good mother and great wife to him. Joy finished high school and went straight to college. Although she partied hard, she stayed focused and got her degree in Business Management and Design. She owned and managed her own small boutique called Cherished Perfection and a small clothing line that she had recently launched called Cherish, named after her daughter. In the midst of this divorce, she was trying to expand her business and open up a few more shops. Her thoughts were interrupted by the tune of Keyshia Cole's "I Ain't Thru." She knew it was her girl Cheryl. Joy and Cheryl had met in middle school when they both attended Charles R. Drew.

Although they had grown up in the same projects, they didn't get close until middle school. Their bond grew stronger over the years, and they had stayed close ever since. She picked up the phone. "Hey, boo! What's up? How are you feeling today?" Cheryl sounded all perky and excited like they haven't talked in years.

"Hey, girl. I'm good," Joy replied in a dry tone.

"No, you are not good. I could hear it all in your voice. Do you want me to come over, so we can talk, or do you want to get lunch or something?" See, although Cheryl and Joy were best friends, Cheryl was also her therapist. Cheryl was twenty-eight and married with two kids by an ex-dope dealer named Chuck. Chuck and Cheryl had been married since she graduated college. It was crazy how they met. She'd always said she would never, ever mess with or marry a nigga who sold drugs, but Chuck made her eat her words when he proposed to her at her graduation. They had been married for a while now. Cheryl was a successful marriage, relationship, and child therapist. She had become really fortunate to kick things off really quickly, and she went and opened her own private practice where she was the boss. Being that Joy was her girl, she gave her and her husband free sessions whenever he would come along. She was always there to listen to Joy and help her out. She knew that her friend needed her, and she was going to make it her business to be there for her. Even though she was calling Joy so she could tell her about her own troubles, she put her own issues aside so she could be there for her friend. Cheryl was always the type of person to put others' problems before her own, and that was what made her a damn good therapist. It wasn't healthy for her, though, because she was going through her own li'l dilemma and didn't know how to get out of it or what to do. She always said that the best therapists were the ones who couldn't seem to follow or take their own advice, and that was so true in her case. She felt it was her duty to be there for her friend to help her though this divorce.

"Naw, Cher I'm good. I'm just tired."

"Look, don't give me that bullshit, Joy. You know I'm always here for you. You're not only my client; you are my best friend," Cheryl said to Joy. She really didn't like for her girl to be going through what she was going through.

"I know, and that's why I love you. You're always there for me when I need you," Joy replied.

"And I love you, too! So with that being said, my schedule is free the rest of the evening. You wanna go have some drinks or something later on? We can have a girls' night. We can bring Keyshia and Sam."

"I was just about to say yes until you said that bitch Sam's name. You know how I feel about that ho. Something is not right about her. She seems real flakey. I don't know what it is about the bitch, but I just don't like her, and you know that," Joy said in a strong tone.

"Joy, don't say that. I told you, she's cool peoples, and besides, you and Keyshia haven't even given her a chance."

"Bitch, don't even go there. You would be the same way, and you were the same way with Tracy and—"

Before Joy could even finish, Cheryl cut her off. "Don't even try that shit. You and I both know why I didn't like that bitch. She was a known ho, and that bitch was just cross action."

They both burst into laughter because they knew it was true as they went down memory lane. Tracy was the ho of the school and always stayed in some drama. Joy and Tracy met in algebra class. One day the class was assigned a group project, and Tracy and Joy began talking. Keyshia and Cheryl never liked Tracy, and anytime she came around, they would either leave or just talk shit about her to her face. Joy constantly tried to get them to come around to her and be cool. One day they were all at the party, and Joy invited Tracy. What Joy had thought was going to be a good night turned out to be the total opposite. Things started okay, but then shit went sour, and Tracy and Keyshia started fighting. It took almost everyone at the party to get Keyshia off of her; she really was trying to kill her. Joy tried to figure out why Keyshia walked up and just punched Tracy in her shit. She figured Keyshia was just drunk and acting an ass. So Joy stopped speaking to Keyshia and Cheryl for about two weeks. She figured Cheryl was down with it, too. Keyshia finally called Joy and told her why she had beat Tracy's ass that night. "Hey, bitch what's up? I know you're still mad at us and all."

"You're damn right I'm pissed with you. Damn, Kesh, you really don't know how to hold your liquor. We always go out, and you start tripping on people for no damn reason. I can understand that you and Cheryl don't like her and the way she carries herself, but damn."

"Look, Joy, fuck you with all that shit you're talking. I fucked that bitch up 'cause I caught her in my fucking car sucking Jimmy's dick. Yeah, that's right. That skanky ass ho was in my damn car that she knew was mine with my fucking dude. So that ho better be lucky I didn't kill her ass. It wasn't the fact that she was fucking with him, but that ho knew that was my motherfucking car, and she still disrespected me. Every time I see that bald-headed bitch, I'mma fuck her up."

The phone got silent as Keyshia was getting mad all over again. Joy was in a state of shock and felt bad about how she was doing her best friend. So they apologized to each other and agreed to never let anything or anyone like that come between them again. A few days after they made up, Joy set Tracy up so Keyshia could wax that ass one more time. This time there was no one there to stop her. From that day on, they all agreed not to let anyone get inside their circle. They would be friendly, but not that friendly, with other chicks. It was supposed to be just the three of them, but once Cheryl and Chuck got married, that changed. Chuck ran into his long-time homie Raymond, and Raymond was married to Samantha. Cheryl and Chuck would double date-or hang with Ray and Samantha from time to time. That's what led Cheryl to begin to vibe with Sam. Joy and Keyshia didn't like her, but they told Cheryl that they would deal with her because of her. But they warned Cheryl if Sam got out of line, they would fuck her up. That's how Sam had come into the picture. So from time to time, they would hang with her. She never tried them or anything, but there was still something fishy about her, and they intended to find out what it was.

"Okay, Cheryl, I get your point, but you need to get my point as well. But okay, we can go out with the bitch!" Joy finally gave in. They both started laughing and then decided to meet up at Chili's to have some drinks and a little to eat.

Chapter Two

THE VERY NEXT DAY, JOY woke up with a banging headache. She and the girls had been out until the wee hours. She didn't have to get up early being that it was the weekend and her daughter was with her farther, so she decided to get out of the house, take a trip to the mall to do some shopping, and pamper herself to help ease her mind.

In the meantime, on the other side of town, Cheryl was driving down Biscayne Boulevard on her way to meet up with a new client of hers when she spotted Chuck's truck at one of the motels. His truck was not hard to miss; he had a black Escalade with 28's, and his plate said "My Toy," so anywhere he went, you would know that it was him. Cheryl had been telling him to change his plates to something that was not so noticeable. She knew the type of past he had and the type people he ran with, and she didn't want anything from his past to come back and hurt him. He had other cars he could drive, but most of the time he always drove that damn truck. Chuck always brushed her off or made some type of excuse or reason as to why he shouldn't have to change it, so she always let him be him.

Now, seeing his truck parked in the lot of a cheap ass motel, she was pretty glad he had never listened to her. Her heart almost went through the floor of her Range Rover when she saw the car that was parked next to his truck. "Naw, this can't be true," she thought out loud to herself. "After I was out drinking and talking all night with this bitch, she had the nerves to be laid up at a fucking motel, fucking my husband!" She screamed while the tears fell down her face. She was in such a daze that she didn't even hear the car horns blowing at her. After a few moments, a few cars went around her and flipped her off. She gathered her thoughts and drove away from the light to make a U-turn. Then she went on the other side of the street from the motel to wait to see when they come out. She called her new client and apologized to her because she would be coming a little late, unless she would want to meet another day. The woman told her no, it was fine; she was about to call her anyway to tell her that she, too, was going to be late. After she hung up the phone, she sat and waited, playing in her mind what she would do and say to them when they came out.

About an hour later, she saw Chuck peek outside the door to make sure the coast was clear before he made his way to his truck. In an instant, Cheryl's body went numb because the whole time she was sitting and waiting, she was hoping and praying it wasn't her husband. Instead of pulling off to follow him, she sat and waited a li'l while longer to see if this bitch was going to come out. Thirty minutes passed, and she never came out. Cheryl looked down at her watch and noticed the time. She had to go so that she could meet up with her new client. Although she wanted her to come out of that room so she could run her ass over, she also had to think about the impression she would give her new client. Besides, Cheryl was always about her money first and foremost. So she decided to leave and get to the bottom of it later.

On her way over to meet her client, she replayed what had happened over and over in her head. Not really sure what her next move would be or how to handle the situation, she was lost and speechless. She wiped her face as she pulled up to her downtown office and checked her face in the mirror to make sure she was presentable. *Hmmp, and I'm supposed to be the one who's an expert in this type of shit. Now look at me. Shit, I don't even know how to handle my own situation,* Cheryl said to herself before she got out of the car to meet her client.

When she entered her office, her assistant greeted her with a stack of phone messages from clients and the people who were working with her to help her launch her website. See, Cheryl was great at what she did. Most people would look at her career as something normal and simple, but she saw more than that. Cheryl felt that what she did and the comfort and help she gave others was something extraordinary. So she graduated college and practiced at a local office, but she decided to open her own firm after seeing that many people preferred to talk to her. She always wondered what she had to offer that was so special to the next human being. After she had stopped one of her clients from killing her kids and then committing suicide, she felt more confident in the work she did and that her profession was needed. So now instead of just meeting up with local clients, Cheryl decided to take her expertise nationwide. Instead of having an advice column in a magazine, she wanted to start her own website dedicated to speaking with clients from all over. Her idea was to have some virtual sessions, and if someone had a general question or problem, they would e-mail her or log onto the website and chat with her instantly.

Her main area of study was in marriage and relationship counseling, but she also worked with kids and young adults at times. Growing up wasn't very easy for her; she had been raped by her stepfather and uncle when she was a child. Living and growing up in a poor/middle-class family, she always wanted to be a shoulder for others because she was able to relate to the things that most people go through. Everything she had gone through in her life made her stronger and helped her move on. She was always there to help anyone who needed her help. People always took her kindness for weakness, and her friends would always tell her that she was a bit too caring for others. Cheryl became that way because she knew how it felt to be alone and have no one there to help you. Now, she was no pushover or doormat—when there was a need for her to give someone the business, you best believe she would handle them. She would fuck a person up with quickness and still have a smile on her face if she felt they were trying to make a fool out of her. At this very moment, after seeing her husband leaving the motel with that bitch she called a friend, she felt that she was being made a fool of. Her thoughts were interrupted as her assistant told her that her new client, Nadine, was waiting for her in her office.

"Okay, thanks! Can you grab me a cup of tea? Thank you so much!" Cheryl said to her.

"Sure, no problem, and you're welcome!"

Cheryl then walked into her office to meet with Nadine. Once she opened the door, there stood a slim five-foot-three, light-skinned woman with some sexy hazel eyes. Her body was to die for, and her skin looked so smooth and creamy. Cheryl was shocked when she saw the frame that stood before her. It was not that her clients were busted ugly or anything, but wow, this woman was not what she had imagined. She looked so amazing. What fool would be so crazy to be giving her problems? Nadine could feel that Cheryl was checking her out, and being that she was a bit shy, she decided to break the awkward silence between them. "Hi. You must be the famous Cheryl?" she asked, extending her hand to properly greet Cheryl.

They shook hands and Cheryl replied, "I wouldn't say famous, but yes, it's me. And you are Nadine, I assume?"

"That would be me. It is a pleasure to finally meet you."

"Same here, and I'm so sorry that I am late. I was a bit caught up with something unexpected."

"Oh no, I understand. There is no need to apologize. I hear that you are worth the wait." They both smiled at the comment Nadine had made, and then Cheryl nodded for her to take a seat. Cheryl then placed her things down and got comfortable in her chair, grabbing her note pad to prepare for their session.

"Okay, so where do we begin? This is my first time coming to a therapist, so excuse me if I seem a bit jumpy or nervous. I am just a bit embarrassed."

"Oh, please do not feel like that. I understand how it may feel. I mean, I have a lot of clients who come in and get nervous. So during any of our sessions, please feel free to let me know if you feel uncomfortable or anything. I will not be pushy or anything. I will let you open up to me when you feel the need. Does that sound okay to you?" Cheryl asked as she smiled and wrote down a few comments on the note pad.

What she said kind of made Nadine feel a little better and confident about what she was doing. "Yes, that sounds great."

"Cool. Now, how would you prefer me to address you? Do you mind if I call you Nadine? And you can call me Cheryl or Cher, by the way."

"Nadine is fine, and thank you."

"Okay, Nadine, before we start, can I ask if your husband is coming late?"

Those words caught Nadine off-guard, and she was back to feeling a little embarrassed. She wanted to tell a lie when she answered instead of the truth. Here she was, sitting in the office for marriage counseling, but she was the only one in her marriage there. She had constantly asked her husband to come with her so that they could get things back on track, but each time he would come up with an excuse about having to work or go on a business trip. This time he just came right out and told her that he was not in the mood for any therapy shit.

"No, Cheryl, my husband will not be joining us this evening. Shit, I don't think he will ever come," she said, forcing herself to laugh.

"That's fine, Nadine. I know it makes your situation that much harder that he is not here, but you never know. He may come around to the idea of it one day. You don't have to feel embarrassed that he is not here. Just look at me as your friend."

"Okay, great. My co-worker told me that you are a great person and the best at what you do, so I won't freak out as much. How does it work when it is just one party?"

Cheryl shifted her body in her chair to get more relaxed and told Nadine to relax and loosen up a bit. She told her she wanted her to feel comfortable and that the more comfortable she was, the easier the process would be.

"Well, as I said, Nadine, whether it's one party or both, I look at it as if I am your friend, and you are just expressing your deepest thoughts and feelings to me. I want you to feel comfortable, so there is really no limit to what you can say and how you express yourself. Just be you. In order for this to help you, you have to want to let out everything that is necessary. I mean, everything—whatever has been on your mind and has been causing the issue, share it if you feel the need to. Because when you hold back emotions, feelings, anger, and things, it only makes you feel worse and makes the situation harder to deal with." She looked over at Nadine, waiting for her to relax and take in all that she had told her before she told her to start wherever she wanted to start.

Nadine was still a bit nervous, so for this session she really didn't open up much. She just told Cheryl bits and pieces about her life and childhood and simple things like that. After talking for about forty-five minutes, they ended the session, and since Nadine was happy that she came, they decided to schedule another session. Cheryl met with two other clients after Nadine, and then her day was pretty much done. She could go home, but being that she had seen her husband leaving the motel earlier, she wanted nothing to do with her house at the moment. She sat at her desk looking over files and looking over all the details of her new project in order to keep her mind off her dilemma. To her surprise, it wasn't working because all she kept seeing was the image of Chuck's ass leaving the fucking motel.

"I can't believe this bitch! Ugh!" she yelled out, knocking all the papers off her desk and beginning to cry. The tears ran like a waterfall; she didn't know what to do. *How in the hell I am able to suggest to people or give advice about what to do about their relationships when here I am, stuck on stupid?"*

After crying for another hour or so, she decided to go home and face the man she had once thought so highly of. As she pulled into the driveway of her five-bedroom home, she put her car in park and sat there for a few moments, taking deep breaths. Once she came inside, her twin boys ran to her. "Mommy, Mommy, you're home! We missed you!" they both yelled as they ran and gave her a big hug. She held on to them so tightly, as though she had not seen them in years. Jerrick and Derrick were five years old, and they were so adorable. Once she finally let them go, they ran back towards the living room where Chuck was sitting watching the evening news.

She wanted so badly to take something and bust his ass in the face, but she always said she would never expose her boys to the violence she was exposed to as a child. Her life was rough, and she never wanted her boys to have to grow up around the same bullshit that she had. Her father and stepfather both used to beat her mama's ass when she was younger as well as hers. So she had to not only watch the abuse but also be abused in the process. All she could think at the moment was, *Damn. All these years, and everything I have done for this motherfucker, and he has the nerves to be sleeping with a bitch I call my friend.*

She walked straight past the living room and up the stairs as if he wasn't even there. Chuck could sense that something was wrong because anytime his wife came home, she would come right over and give him a kiss that sent chills through his body. Now she walked in the house and didn't even acknowledge that he was there. He figured maybe she had had a bad day, and he didn't want to bother her, so he continued to watch the news. After giving the boys a bath and putting them to bed, Cheryl went and ran herself a hot bubble bath, grabbed a glass of Moscato, and lay back and relaxed. She let out a long sigh of relief. She had begun to drift off in a dream, and then her perfect moment was interrupted as Chuck entered the restroom.

"Damn, so I can't join you, baby?" She wanted to curse his ass out so badly, but she was too tired to even hear what lie he had to tell her.

"I'm just tired, Chuck, that's all. I had a long day, and I just didn't want to be bothered. That's all."

He could tell she was a bit annoyed by the tone in her voice, so instead of even responding, he leaned over, gave her a kiss, and just left the bathroom and went to the bedroom. His cell started to ring, and when he looked at the caller ID, his heart dropped. Without another thought, he answered the phone in a hurry, hoping she didn't hear it ring.

"What's good?" Chuck spoke into the phone while watching the door to make sure Cheryl didn't come in the room and catch him.

"I just wanted to tell you goodnight and that I had a good time today. And don't forget about tomorrow! Love ya!" the voice on the other end of the phone said before hanging up without even letting Chuck get out another word. He didn't know if Cheryl had heard his phone ring or not, so to make it less obvious, Chuck continued to talk, pretending he was on the phone talking to Ray about a basketball game.

After he hung up his fake conversation, Cheryl entered the room. The aroma from her Victoria's Secret fragrance that she bathed her body in smelled so delicious, it had him wanting to eat. Cheryl knew that he loved when she smelled so good, and she could tell by the look in eyes he wanted to tear that pussy up. She was mad at herself because looking at his sexy brown skin and his medium-build frame, she wanted him to get that pussy. He looked over at her as she walked across the room in her Vicky's Secret lingerie that showed enough of her skin to make him want to rip everything else off her. Her skin tone complemented the red she wore, and it made his dick jump. He began to lick his lips, and she could feel her pussy get moist. She was trying so hard to fight the temptation, but the way he looked at her and the way she was looking at those sexy, thick lips, all she could do was imagine him feasting on that juicy pussy of hers. Cheryl didn't want him to know that she wanted him as badly as he wanted her, so she sat down on her side of the bed and lotioned her body. Then she sat back on the bed, got under the covers, and turned on the TV. About five minutes later, she felt Chuck's hand rubbing her inner thigh. She tried to play like she didn't feel it, but the feeling was so soft and good. Chuck began to kiss and suck on her neck, sending chills all through her body. He continued to kiss all over her, and the tension in her body began to loosen up as his kisses got lower and lower. Damn. She wanted to push his ass off her, but it felt so damn good.

The next thing she knew, he was kissing on her inner thighs, and then he made his way deeper between her legs. Cheryl tensed up at first, but then she let out a sigh and relaxed her body as the kisses got closer to her middle. She arched her back and let out a soft moan as he began to plant soft kisses on her clit, teasing it with his soft lips. He could tell she was ready because her pussy was dripping wet. It was so wet it made his dick stand straight up. He pulled her down closer to his face and began to suck on her clit and taste her juices. Each time his mouth touched her clit, she moaned louder and louder. Cheryl's thoughts were no longer on what she was upset about; all she could think about was the good feeling that she was feeling on her pussy. Chuck sucked and pulled and licked on her pussy, and then he teased her and stuck two fingers inside her. Each time he stuck them in her, he could feel her warm, dripping pussy grip his fingers. That shit turned him on more and more. Her pussy was soaking wet and warm, and it felt so damn good. He wanted this feeling on his dick. Her body started trembling as he continued to feast on that juicy nectar of hers. In between licks and sucks he told her, "Cum all over my face, baby. I feel this pussy cumming. Damn, this pussy tastes so good. Umm, I want you to cum all in my mouth, baby." Cheryl was speechless; she was unable to say a word. It was feeling so damn good. All she could do was moan and move her body. Before she knew it, her body went to shaking, and he went to sucking.

"Ooooh, Chuck, baby, I'm cum-cum-cumming, baby. Oh my gosh, it feels so good. Eat this pussy, baby. I'm cumming, baby."

As she continued to moan and talk, her body shook uncontrollably, and at that moment she was cumming all over Chuck's face. Her juices flowed like a river, and he enjoyed every moment of it. He was ready to feel that warm juicy pussy, so he turned her around, but to his surprise she wasn't ready for that. She instructed him to lie on his back. Then she positioned herself so that her ass was in the air and her face towards his throbbing dick. She began to tease him and lick on the head of his dick at first. Each time she licked the tip of the head, she watched his dick jump, and that made her pussy even wetter. Cheryl then took her lips and wrapped them around just the head and began to suck the life out of it. Chuck was going crazy as she teased his manhood. His toes were curling, and his eyes were rolling in the back of his head. Right when he thought she was about to stop, she took all nine inches in her mouth, and that sent chills up his body. He could feel her throat muscles as she went deeper and took it all in.

"Damn, baby, oh my god," Chuck yelled as she held his dick deep in her throat. Cheryl then came up slowly and began to suck on his dick like it was a big, juicy pop sickle.

"Damn, baby. Damn, Cheryl. Damn, it feels so good, baby. Umm, baby, you're treating daddy's dick good."

The moaning and talking he was doing was driving her wild; her pussy was leaking wet all over the bed as she sucked on his juicy dick. Cheryl was in her own zone. She loved when he would moan and talk. Her pussy was throbbing and ready to feel that dick. She stopped sucking, climbed on top of him, and straddled herself around his dick, teasing him by only squatting down on the head.

"Ooooh shit, girl, this pussy so warm and wet. Don't tease me, baby, let me feel all of this pussy. I wanna stroke this pussy baby," Chuck moaned as she continued to ride only the head, making him go crazy. Then she tightened her pussy muscles and squatted down slowly, taking all of it in. As she slid down on his dick, she let out a moan.

"Umm, damn, Chuck. This dick's so good."

She began to ride him up and down, slow then fast. She then turned so she could ride him backwards. Once she was turned all the way around, she bounced up and down on his dick, and he smacked her fat ass each time she came down. They were both moaning and panting out of control, and she felt herself about to explode all over his dick.

"Baby, I'm about to cum. I want you to cum with me, baby. Ooh shit, Chuck, this dick feels sooooo good."

"Yes, baby, and this pussy is so warm. Cum on this dick, baby. I'm cumming, Cher. I'm cumm—ahhh…"

They both exploded, and she could feel all his nut shoot up inside of her. It felt so good and warm. Both of their juices mixed together as she stayed straddled on his dick. Both of their bodies went limp. She lay on top of him for a while, and then she watched him drift off to sleep. She got up, cleaned herself up, and went to bed.

Chapter Three

THE NEXT MORNING, CHERYL GOT the boys ready for school, and then she got dressed for work. To her surprise, when she came downstairs, Chuck was already gone. He left a note on the counter that read, "Sorry, babe. I have an early meeting. See you tonight. Oh, I really enjoyed last night! Love, Chuck." Cheryl took the note and placed it in the trash.

"Oh yeah, I bet you did have to go. Ugh," she thought out loud. After getting the boys off to school, she decided to call Joy and Keyshia to see if they wanted to get some brunch. "Hey, bitch, what's up?" Joy greeted her as she answered the phone. People always wondered why they talked to each other like that, but it was something between them. No one else would dare disrespect them like that.

"Nothing much. Are you busy? Did you and Kesh want to go have some brunch?"

"No, my day is pretty free today, so I'm down. Let me call Kesh and see where she's at. Where do you want to go?"

"Um, I really don't know what I want to eat." They both let out a chuckle.

"Well, while you decide, I'm going to call Keyshia and let her know and then call you back, okay?"

"Okay, deal!"

After they hung up, she wondered if she should tell them about Chuck. Part of her wanted to confide in her friends, but the other part wasn't ready for the responses she would get. So after about a good thirty minutes, she spoke back with Joy, and they decided to go to the Waffle House. Now, that was one of their favorite spots because their damn waffles were so damn good. Once they all arrived there, they greeted each other in the parking lot and then headed inside to order. As they sat there and waited for their food, they were just quiet and looking at each other. Joy decided to break the silence. "Damn, why y'all bitches so damn quiet? What's really good? Shit, I'm the one going through it, and both of y'all look more depressed than me."

Keyshia and Joy both started laughing. Then Keyshia said, "Well, ho, you know damn well I ain't depressed. I'm just tired as hell. Shit, I didn't get in the house till like five this morning. Then here comes your ass calling, talking 'bout some damn brunch. But a bitch hungry, so excuse me if I'm not my normal self."

They started laughing again. Then both of them stopped as they noticed tears running down Cheryl face. They were shocked to see her like this. "What's the matter, boo?" Kesh and Joy both said in a concerned sincere voice.

Cheryl was still unsure whether to tell them or not, so she decided to tell them parts of the story, not all of it just yet. She was still afraid of being judged. "Chuck is cheating on me!" She could no longer hold back the tears. She was fighting so hard not to break down. But the pain and betrayal she was feeling took over, and she began to cry harder. Keyshia and Joy both were shocked because never in a million years would they guess that Cheryl would be going through anything. She was always chipper and upbeat; she was the person you would go to cry and let out your feelings to.

"Damn. You sure? I can't believe this. You two seemed so happy," Keyshia said.

"Hmmp, yeah. You would think that and so did I. I guess I'm seeing something different 'cause I thought my marriage was great. I just can't believe that I am going through the same shit I supposedly help others with. It makes me feel like I shouldn't be a fucking therapist."

"Cut that shit out, Cher. You always said the best therapists are those who can't follow their own advice or help themselves. Besides, just 'cause you are a therapist, it doesn't make you exempt from going through shit. You're only human. You can't always have the answers. And that is what you have us here for—to help you when you need it. You're always looking out and helping others, but you always forget about the most important person: yourself. Sometimes Superwoman needs to be saved, too," Joy told her as she leaned over to grab her hand.

Keyshia got up to get some napkins, so she could wipe her face. Thank goodness they were in the back in the corner, and no one could see her breaking down. Keyshia was shocked and puzzled as to how in the hell this happened or how did she know. So once she sat back at the table, she asked, "Not to jump so far ahead, but how you know?"

Cheryl wiped her face and cleared her throat before she began to speak. "Well, I was headed to the office to meet up with this new client, and I spotted his truck at a motel on Biscayne." She choked up again and started crying. All Joy and Keyshia could do was sit there and look in a state of shock.

"Damn, bitch, are you serious?" Keyshia said, shaking her head in disbelief. They all sat in silence for a few more moments, and Cheryl wiped her eyes. She planned not to give them all the details about who he was with because she knew that she would not hear the end of it. Out of the blue, Joy's dramatic ass burst into tears. Keyshia looked at her like she was fucking crazy. For Joy, it just brought back all the drama she was going through in her life, and she felt bad that she hadn't realized that her best friend needed her.

"I'm sorry, Cheryl. I feel so bad. I have been being a selfish bitch, pouring out all my problems when you really needed someone to be there for you."

"No, don't feel that way at all. Neither you nor I could have known something like this was going to happen to me. And besides, I am just finding out myself. So don't ever feel that you are being selfish, and you know we have to be here for each other. I'm just as shocked as you are. I mean, damn, this motherfucker could have been more discreet with it. He's with the bitch all on Biscayne and shit, knowing that I take that way to the office at times," Cheryl said as she continued to wipe her face.

"At least you know that bitch he's fucking is a cheap bitch. Shit, he took that ho to a cheap ass motel on Biscayne!" Keyshia tried to make them see some humor out of the situation. She was never really good at this type of comforting stuff because she was single, and she planned on being that way for a long time. Her last relationship was with this guy named Alex. It was all good in the beginning, and she changed all her ways for him. But then she came home and found him in bed with the next bitch, and she tried to kill both of them. After that, she promised herself that she would never trust another nigga again. Joy and Cheryl both had tried talking to her and telling her that one man can't define what all men are about and that she needed to slow down and change her ways. But she stuck to her motto: "Fuck a nigga and his feelings." Keyshia was out here to get what she could get out of a nigga, and that was money and a good fuck. They always warned her that her day would come, so she needed to be careful of the shit she was doing.

They both looked at her and laughed. It was good that they saw some humor in what she said. Although they were both hurt, it was good to laugh through the pain. "So what are you gonna do bitch? You going to tell his sorry ass what you saw and then leave his ass before it gets worse?" Joy asked, checking her make up.

Cheryl was stuck because she really loved her husband. This was the first time something like this had happened, and there had been no signs, so she felt that there was some type of explanation. Before she made a rash decision, she wanted to hear him out. Now, she knew once she said that to them, she was going to hear all types of negative feedback. Before she could even speak, Keyshia said, "You don't even have to answer that question 'cause I can see the answer written all over your face. Bitch, you want to give his ass another chance, and we all know how you are with your shit about 'everybody deserves a second chance.' Then again, who am I to judge? As you would tell me or anybody else, you have to follow your heart. No one can make this choice for you. I may not agree with it, but I will support whatever decision you decide to make. I me—"

Before she could finish another word, Joy cut her off. "Bitch, please. A second chance is the reason I am in the mess I'm in now. Fuck that. His ass doesn't deserve shit but to get served. I mean, shit, like you said, you do this for a living. You give bitches advice on a daily basis about what they should do in their relationships. And now look at you; you can't even follow your own damn advice."

"But like she said before, Joy, the best therapist is one who can't follow her own advice. And let's be real, ho. You're in this boat because you were hard-headed. After the damn second time his ass did it, we told you to leave his ass alone. But no. You stayed, talking 'bout you didn't want to break up your family and all that other bullshit females like you are always screaming. So neither you nor I can judge her. We just have to be here for her. So let's just do that," Keyshia told Joy.

"Yeah, I feel you, Dr. Phil-ass bitch," Joy replied, and they all burst out laughing. Cheryl was prepared for this; she had known exactly what her friends would say. That's why she really didn't want to tell them. She didn't give them too many details. She sat there and didn't say much. After that, they all ate, said their goodbyes, and went on their separate ways.

As Cheryl was pulling in the driveway, her phone rang. When she looked down and saw that it was Samantha, she thought about whether she should answer it or not. She sent her to voicemail, but she called right back. Not really in the mood to talk to Sam, Cheryl picked up with a really sour tone. "Yeah, hello?"

"Well, damn. Is that how you answer all your calls? I would hate to be one of your clients if you sounded like that all the time."

Cheryl really wanted to go off on her ass, but she decided this was not the time. Instead, she would be nice to the bitch. "I'm sorry, girl. Today is just not one of the best days. But what's up?"

"Damn, I guess that is a virus that is going around because today is not one of my best days either. That's why I called you."

Damn, everybody wanna call me when their ass is going through some shit. When is a bitch going to call me to see how I'm doing? Fuck! Did I really pick the best profession? These bitches and their problems are getting on my damn nerves, Cheryl thought to herself, letting out a long sigh to try and calm her nerves. She was already very pissed off about the shit with her.

"No, now I feel bad that I called you, and you have your own issues you're going through. I will be okay," Sam said. She wanted so badly to tell Cheryl what was up, but she didn't know what her reaction would be. Now that she knew her day was going badly, she decided not to tell her.

"Girl, I do this shit for a living, so it's no biggie. So tell me, what's good?"

"Are you sure?"

"Bitch, I said yeah. Now what's up, before I change my mind?" They both started laughing. Sam didn't know what to say or where to start, so she just told her what else was bothering her.

"Girl, I think Ray's ass is cheating on me. Well, fuck that. I am pretty sure this nigga's cheating."

Now either this was a virus that was going around, or this bitch was just trying to cover up her own fucking dirt. Here she was, pissed that she had caught her husband cheating with Sam, and now Sam was supposedly going through the same thing. But hey, this was the type of work she was used to, so it was nothing new to her. She shook off her thoughts and got into her role. Besides, she needed to know as much as possible.

"Are you serious? How did you find out? Did you catch him in the act?"

"Dang, is this what you drill your clients with? I am scared of you." They both started to laugh. "I have to keep myself laughing, so I won't keep crying. My damn eyes are killing me from all this damn crying. No, I didn't catch him in the act, but I saw the signs and figured something was going on. He'd come home later than normal, take a shower, and go straight to sleep. Then when I wanted to have sex, he'd turn me down. Or if we did have sex, it's like he did it just to keep me from asking him. It was all just crazy. I was tired of assuming and guessing, so I went through his phone. I thought about all the stuff you said 'bout 'if you go searching, be prepared for what you might find.' I wasn't with all that, waiting until what's in the dark to come to the light. Shit, I needed to know! And I...I..."She couldn't even finish; she broke down crying.

Cheryl felt a little bit bad in a way because of the thoughts she was having, but she knew Sam needed a friend and a shoulder to lean on. She really didn't have much to do, so she decided to invite her to meet her somewhere, so she could talk to her about it. They agreed to meet at the park near her house since they had already eaten lunch. Once she got there, she spotted Sam. She didn't look like her normal perky self—really, she looked a hot mess. Her hair was a mess, and her eyes were swollen from all the crying she had been doing. As they walked up to each other, Cheryl held out her arms to give Sam a hug. They embraced each other for a few moments and then found a bench to sit on, so they could talk more. Cheryl was shocked because she had never seen her like this before, and she was kind of hurt for her. Although she had her own issues, she decided to put them aside and deal with them later when everyone's guards were down.

"Damn, girl, you look a hot mess. I'm sorry to say it like this, but I have never seen you look this bad. I mean, this is really not you. So talk to me. What happened? What did you find? Don't tell me his ass got a bitch pregnant, too? I'll be damned if he does. This will be some crazy shit."

"No, it's not that deep. It's just the fact of me fining out and knowing that I have changed my ways, and I am faithful to this nigga, and he has the nerve to try me like this. Girl, he has been fucking with this bitch for over a year." Sam got more pissed off as she thought about it. She knew she wasn't a saint, but she hated the idea of herself getting played. She wasn't about to tell

Cheryl that she still had her own little hidden agenda, but she was trying to change, and this was making it harder for her to do that.

"How do you know all of this? Did you talk to the bitch?"

"No, I tried calling the bitch, but she never answered, as if she knew it was me or something."

"Well, what do you now, and how much do you know?" Cheryl was getting kind of pissed 'cause this bitch knew she wasn't all Mrs. Innocent. Her track record wasn't so clean. That bitch was foul, too, and she knew it. Part of her didn't want to help her for that reason, but she wasn't that type of person—or at least she wasn't that type of bitch until it was necessary. And besides, she needed to hear this bitch out before she put her plan into motion.

"Well, like I said, I had been noticing all of the changes for a while. So the other day, I told him that we needed to talk and that I wanted him to try and come home early so we could. He seemed kind of agitated with the fact that I kept pressing him about the whole cheating thing. So his tone of voice wasn't pleasant when he told me okay. He stormed out of the door without so much as a 'see you later.'"

She began to sniffle and wipe her tears as she continued her story. "I was pissed. I wanted to go after his ass and give him the business, but I decided that I would save all my rage for later. The bitch left so fast, he forgot his phone. A part of me wanted to run and give it to him because he hadn't pulled out of the garage yet, but then there was that devil in me, laughing that sneaky laugh. So I went through it, and girl did I get an eye-full.

The bitch had just texted him that morning and said they needed to talk 'cause this was going to have to come to an end 'cause it wasn't right, and people could end up getting hurt."

She paused for a moment so that she could calm herself down, so she wouldn't cry. "I was like, 'Okay, since the bitch wants to call it off, I will think about giving him another chance 'cause I have done my share of cheating.' I'm thinking this nigga loves me and wants to stay with me, but the next text I read is him telling this bitch that he loves her and that he told her that he would leave me—just say the word, and it's done. This tired ass nigga even had the nerve to tell the bitch that I don't even turn him on anymore; he's only with me 'cause of the kids and to pass time. If he has to start over, he wants it to be with her. This fucker says he is not even in love with me, and he regrets he let it even go on this long. At first he thought it was a phase he was going through, but this is something he really wants with this other bitch." She could no longer hold back the tears; now she was crying uncontrollably.

Cheryl was shocked because the Sam she knew never let herself go like this. But then again, what did she really know about Sam? She and Sam had met through their husbands. Sam's husband Ray and Chuck had gone to high school and college together. Ray had moved to West Virginia to play football, but he ended up getting hurt and came back to Miami. He ran into Chuck one day at the mall, and they caught up on all the old times and then introduced their wives to each other. Ray and Chuck had both had a threesome back in college with Sam, and Chuck was shocked when he saw that they had gotten married.

Cheryl never knew that Chuck had known Sam prior to their first meeting. She thought that Chuck met her through Ray because it was his wife. So as time passed and they all hung out together, they got closer and went on double dates. Then Cheryl introduced Sam to Keyshia and Joy, being that Sam didn't have many friends. They all hung out from time to time, but Joy and Keyshia always had a bad vibe about her. Cheryl had always took up for her, but little did she know this same bitch had fucked her husband. There were so many times that Sam wanted to tell Cheryl that she had already known Chuck, but she was afraid it would mess up their relationship, and she didn't want to betray her husband.

"It hurts so badly to know that I'm in a marriage all alone. I never knew he felt this way. I don't know what to do." She continued to cry.

Cheryl looked at Sam, who was crying with her face buried in her chest. She really didn't know what to say to the woman who was fucking her husband. She wanted so badly to beat her ass in that park. All she could think of was the image of her fucking car parked next to his at the damn motel. *And now this ho has the nerve to come to me 'cause her fucking husband is cheating on her? This bitch must have lost her damn mind. Damn, it's really a grimy world. Bitches can be fucking your man and come around you like nothing ever happened.*

Cheryl was starting to get pissed all over again, but she had to stay calm; she had something in store for Mrs. Samantha. So she played her role of a caring friend and therapist. "Sam, I can only imagine how you are feeling right now, but trust me, I can relate to everything you are feeling. I see this in women every day. We as humans are going to go through hurt, and that is just the way life is. What you have to figure out is what you plan to do. In this case, I can tell you what I tell the rest because it seems to me you're in a place where you are not wanted and haven't been wanted for so long. The fucked up part about it is that for all this time, you thought you were the one, and only now you are finding out that you aren't."

Cheryl let out a long sigh because it was hard to pretend to care for the enemy, but then again part of her felt sorry for her. Now she was wondering if this was the reason Sam had decided to sleep with Chuck. Chuck and Ray were such good friends, and this could hurt Ray. She didn't know what she was even going to do about her situation with them. Her heart was hurting, and she wondered if Chuck felt the same way about her that Ray felt about Sam. *Damn, what if he feels the same way?* she thought to herself.

Her phone rang, and she felt a moment of relief. She looked down and saw that it was Chuck calling. She didn't feel like being bothered with his ass because if she heard his voice, she would fuck Sam up since she was the closet one to her reach.

"Cheryl, if you have to take that, you can. I just needed to get that out of my system. You know I don't have many friends or people I can trust, but I do appreciate you being here for me."

"No worries. I am glad that I can be here for you. So what are your plans?"

"If I tell you, you're going to think I am a fool."

"Not at all. That isn't my style. I can't judge you because at the end of the day, whatever choice you make, you have to live with it. I can only tell you my opinion, and that's all. I can't tell you or make you do anything you don't desire to do." From Sam's response, Cheryl knew that Sam was going to say that she was going to give him another chance. And she felt that part of Sam wanted to give him another chance because Sam was fucking Chuck and she had fucked all kinds of other people, too. Bitches like that felt they were one up on everyone else, and their secrets were safe…but not for long.

"Thanks, I appreciate that. See, that's why I called you. I knew you wouldn't judge me. I just feel that since I have done the same thing to him before, I should give him a chance. I know two wrongs don't make a right, but I just don't want to lose him and have to start over and break up our family."

There was that famous line women love to use! Cheryl had heard her clients say this very same thing so many times, and she always wondered why. Now it made her wonder: Should she do the same? Was there some kind of satisfaction in it? She knew there wasn't, but damn, she was in the same boat she saw many women in—settled with a husband, career, and kids, and now the family had to be torn apart. It was something she would have to think about. Here she was, saying women shouldn't feel a certain way in this situation, but now she wasn't really sure if she could practice what she preached.

"Look, as I said, I can't judge you on what you decide to do, but you are doing the very thing that most women do. What I don't understand is the justification for doing it. I mean, everyone says, 'Well, okay, if he cheats I'm going to do the same'—or, in your case, since you have done it to him, it's okay for him to do it to you. All I can tell you is that two wrongs don't make a right, and don't settle for anything. I understand you have a family, and trust me, it is hard tearing down something you worked long and hard to build. But you have to know that just as you built this, you can build again. To be truly real with you, follow your heart. If you truly love him, fight for what you feel is right. If deep in your heart you feel it's worth fighting for, you just have to make sure what you are fighting for wants to be won," Cheryl said.

"I hear you, but shit, it's hard, and it's not like we're getting younger. I just feel that I should accept the world for what it is. Cher, I know that you do this for a living, and you understand what I am going through, but what I don't understand is how can you build something new when you have been hurt."

"You are right. Yes, you have been hurt, but can you really say or know that you are going to get hurt if you start over? If you are willing to take a risks by staying, what's wrong with taking a risk and leaving? You will never know unless you try. It's just like when you first met Ray and got married to him. You didn't know if he was going to hurt you or not, but you took the chance to trust and believe that he wouldn't."

"Exactly my point! And look where it has led me. So what is the purpose of even starting over to be let down again? If that is the case, I might as well take my chances with what I have."

Cheryl felt where she was coming from; she didn't want her to want to stay for the wrong reasons. But then again, she really didn't give a damn; this bitch wasn't a saint. "I understand where you are coming from, and that is why I said that this is just my opinion and that I cannot judge you on what you decide to do. Just remember, whatever you decide is something that you have to live with. Women say that they want to do what is best for them and the kids, but you have to think really hard about the choice because it can hurt the kids as well. You have to be sure that you are thinking of your children's best interest as well. What you need to do is just take some time to think about what you really want to do. If trying to stay is what you want, go for it. No matter which risk you decide to take, just make sure you are prepared for whatever comes out of it."

Cheryl's phone rang again. This time it was her assistant, and she made a mental note to call her soon as she finished.

"Thank you, Cheryl, I will do just that. It's just really crazy and hard, but I know I can make it. I appreciate this, and I am sorry for interrupting your day with this. But I needed someone to talk to."

"Not a problem at all. It's cool. I do have to leave because now my assistant is blowing me up. She normally doesn't call when I am not planning on coming in. Maybe we can get together later this week. Take care, and call me if you need anything."

"Thanks. I will, and you take care, too. I love you, girl."

They hugged each other and headed to their cars. As soon as Cheryl got in her truck, she started to call her assistant, but her phone rang again, and it was her.

"I was just dialing the office back. Sorry I didn't answer the first time. I was with a client. What's up?"

"I'm sorry to bother you, but you know that client you met with the other day? She is back. I know that you are not supposed to meet with her, but she insisted on seeing you. I tried telling her you are not in the office today, but she would not leave."

Cheryl let out a long sigh. *What have I gotten myself into? Just when I thought I was headed home,* she thought to herself. "Okay, tell her I will be over in an hour or so. I have to go by the house and shower and grab a few things. Thanks. And it's no worries about calling me. See you later," Cheryl said. Then they hung up.

Chapter Four

ABOUT AN HOUR OR SO later, Cheryl was headed to meet Nadine at her office. When she left the house, Chuck wasn't home, so she tried calling his cell. It went straight to voicemail. "Hey, it's me. I've been trying to call you to let you know that I will be home later. I have to meet up with this new client of mine. The kids are at my aunt's house. Just call me when you're free."

She was a little pissed that he was not answering her calls. She had tried calling him over five times. She decided to take her usual route to the office, being that there was not much traffic. She really wanted to get back home to relax, but she was in for a surprise as she rode past the same motel and saw Chuck's truck speeding out of the parking lot. He was driving like he was pissed because you could hear his tires.

"Ain't this 'bout a bitch! Ugh!" Cheryl screamed, hitting her hand on the steering wheel. She was so pissed. She really didn't know what to do. Without any further hesitation, she got to the light and made a U-turn. By the time she got back to the motel, they were both gone. She parked in the parking lot to take a moment to gather her thoughts. Cheryl was still shocked that they were so bold and open with their sneaking around. "I promise I'm going to fuck both of them up. Watch."

Before she knew it, tears were racing down her face. She was so hurt. As she sat and cried, her phone began to ring. It was her assistant. She knew that she was late to meet with this new client, but she really wasn't in the mood. She picked up her phone quickly and told her assistant that she was a few minutes away and hung up. As soon as she hung up, it rang again. She thought it was her assistant calling back, so she didn't even look at the phone as she picked it up.

"I said that I will be there in a few minutes. If she can't wait, then tell her to leave! Shit!"

"Damn, baby, what's wrong with you?" said the sexy, familiar voice on the other end of the phone. "Who is stressing my wife out and rushing her to get to them? I told you that you need to take a vacation, a getaway from all these people and their problems. You can't have them stressing you out like this."

Before he could finish, she cut him off. "Really, that sounds like a great idea. I should get away from everybody and their damn problems."

Her tone was very blunt and she seemed pissed off. Chuck could sense her attitude and was puzzled as to why she was talking to him with such anger in her voice. "Well damn, I know that you're pissed at whoever keep calling you, but why are you speaking to me in that tone, Cher? This is the shit I'm talking about. You let these people piss you off and then take it out on the world. Well…"

She was getting angrier as he spoke, and she cut him off. "Look, I don't want to hear shit about my clients or anybody else pissing me off. I'm pissed off and sick of your lying, cheating ass. That's who the fuck I'm mad at. Since you think you can diagnose me, nigga, you listen to sprint and think about why the fuck you make me sick."

Before he could say another word, she hung up. He sat there puzzled, wondering why the hell she was tripping. The last time she really went off on him and he didn't know why, she was pregnant. Chuck was wondering if she was having another baby, but then it dawned on him where she said she was headed. "Fuck! She probably saw me leaving the motel. Oh shit, I hope she only saw me. Damn, damn, damn!" he said, slapping his hands on his head. Now all he could think about was what he was going to do. If she really found out his secret, his family would be ruined. He had been trying to end it for a while now, but it was still going on.

His phone interrupted his thoughts. A half-smile came on his face because he thought it was Cheryl calling him back, but to his surprise it wasn't. It was the person who was about to ruin his family. The sight of the number pissed him off, so he picked up the phone with a nasty attitude.

"Look, now is not the time. I cannot and do not feel like talking to you right now."

"What the hell is your problem? Lately, you have been tripping. We just left each other, and you didn't seem agitated when you were all up in me. So what changed since then?" The person on the other end seemed a bit upset. They had just had some great sex, and now Chuck was acting strange. But Chuck didn't give a fuck about what they had just shared; all he cared about was losing his wife and kids over this bullshit.

"What changed was I think my fucking wife saw us leaving the motel!" he yelled through the phone. Everything went silent; you could hear nothing but each of them breathing. Neither one of them really knew what to say because if she had seen them, there was not much they could say. Chuck got tired of just holding the phone. This motherfucker was the reason Cheryl was pissed at him in the first place, so he decided to end the conversation.

"So now you have nothing to say, huh? I kept telling your ass that we had to end this shit before someone caught us. But no because you have your own issues and want out of your marriage, you want to make me leave mine as well. I told you when this shit started that it was a mistake and just a phase. I don't want to give up my family, and I know that I can't have my family and you. So the choice I want to make is my family. I'm sorry, but I'm serious this time. This is it, no more. So let's just leave it where it's at." He didn't even give the person a chance to say anything; he just hung up the phone.

Cheryl was livid, but she didn't want Nadine to see her breakdown, so she had to pull herself together before she walked in her office. As soon as she walked in, she saw Nadine sitting on the chair, crying her eyeballs out. Cheryl felt her pain and wanted to help her so badly.

"Hi, Nadine, I'm sorry I'm late. What's the matter, sweetheart?" Cheryl went over to her desk to get her some tissue and handed it to her, so she could clean her face. Nadine had her head down, and when she lifted her head to get the tissue and looked at Cheryl, her eyes were bloodshot red. She looked like she had been crying for days. "Oh, sweetheart, what happened?"

Nadine sniffled then wiped her face. "Hi. I'm sorry. I know our meeting wasn't until a few days from now, but I really needed someone to talk to. I don't know what else to do."

"It's okay. What's going on?"

"My husband left for a business trip yesterday, and when I called his room today, a woman answered the phone. I was stunned. I just hung up the phone. I really didn't know what to say or do. Then later on, he called me, and I told him that I had been trying to call him and about what happened. He got all upset and defensive and said that he was getting sick of me and this cheating shit that I am accusing him of. Cheryl, I know I can overreact at times, but I know that I called the right number."

Nadine began to break down and cry again. Cheryl felt bad for her because there was a possibility that she could be right about her husband. Then again, she could just be paranoid due to the fact that he is always missing in action.

"Nadine, calm down. Just take a deep breath and relax. I can understand how you may be feeling, being that he is always gone away on business trips, but you can't take yourself through this. You have no proof. Now, it is very normal for a woman to have that gut-feeling that something isn't right, but for me, I always feel that there is something that brings that feeling on."

"What do you mean by that?"

"What I mean is that normally, some women get insecure and suspect things if they have previously cheated on or are still cheating on their spouse. Then you have the ones who get that gut-feeling when he starts changing up his routine and how treats her. You even have women get this way when they have gained a few pounds and don't feel as attractive as they used to, and they think that their spouse is going to go out and get something better. There are all types of scenarios that women think of that make them feel that something isn't right. I am not saying that either of these are you, and I am not saying that what you are thinking is wrong. I always say you have to hope for the best but prepare for the worst."

She paused for a moment to try and sense what Nadine was thinking. Nadine had stopped crying for a moment and was playing with her fingers as if she had something to say. Cheryl never pressured any of her clients; she always gave them room to make the choice to express whatever they felt was needed to say. Nadine knew deep down that Cheryl had hit it right on-point and that she was very much like those women whom she had described. She never thought she would have to expose her secret, but she always knew that what was in the dark would eventually have to come to the light.

"Well…it's tough for me to say it, but you are right. The reason I am so insecure and afraid he is cheating is because about a year or two ago, I had an affair." Just the mention of it made her sick to her stomach, but she put her head down and continued the story. Cheryl was a little shocked by what she heard.

"I had gained a few pounds, and things weren't that great between us. At that time, I was a mess, and I needed some attention and affection, something I was lacking at home. So I met this chick at the gym, and we started hanging and working out together. One day she told me that she found me very attractive. I told her that I was married and that I was not into women, and she backed off for the moment. Then one day we went out, and he was out of town on yet another business trip. She invited me to stay at her house, so I wouldn't be alone." Tears filled her eyes as she continued the story. "I was a bit skeptical about staying, but I really didn't want to be alone that night. So we went to her place, and we had a few more drinks. After I took a shower to relax, she came in the guest room and began kissing all over my body. Wow, this is crazy. I swore I would never tell anyone this secret, but it felt so good what she was doing to me. She made sure that she caressed, licked, and sucked all the right parts of my body. I had not felt like that in such a long time, and I really needed it."

Nadine went further into the story, and Cheryl was shocked but turned on at the same time by the way she described how they had sex and how the chick had made her feel that night. Cheryl wasn't into women and never had been, but damn, she was curious to know how in the hell a chick could suck and lick your pussy and make you feel that way. Cheryl was surprised and really didn't know what to say because she had never had a situation like this before. Nadine was silent for a moment and felt that she had unloaded a bomb on her therapist, but that was just the least of her secrets. Instead of spilling all of it, she decided to save the rest for another day.

"Okay, so I can understand why you may be feeling the way you are feeling, and that is normal. You cheated, and now you are afraid that he will do or is doing the same to you. Although this is very awkward, I don't know much to say. I mean, it was a woman—is that really cheating? I mean, you know men love to see two women fucking each other. So I doubt he would be mad at all. He probably would be made that he wasn't invited," she said jokingly.

"I'm just joking; I wanted to make you smile," Cheryl told her. "Well, let me ask you this: Does he know what happened?" Cheryl asked as she jotted down a few notes.

Nadine answered the question quickly. "No! No one knows about this—well, except you now. I promised I would never tell anyone. It was too embarrassing," Nadine said in a soft, scared tone of voice. Cheryl could tell that it was something that Nadine wad embarrassed about, but at the same time, it seemed as if Nadine had never really wanted it to end.

Cheryl was tired of guessing and just went straight to the point. "So tell me something. Do you regret that you let it end with her?"

Nadine was surprised that she had asked her that question, but she knew that it was obvious; the way she spoke about her gave the impression that she still wanted it. "I won't say I regret it, but I am a little upset that I let it go. See, each time I was with her, she made me feel like a queen. She treated me so well. Besides the fact of our always having sex, she was always there to comfort me and meet my every need. The way she took the time to listen to me and my needs made the sex a bonus. Cheryl, there have been times I have thought about leaving my husband just so I could be with her, but then I had to realize that it was not the right thing to do and that people would look at me differently. I never wanted anyone to judge me or have anything negative to say, so I cut it off. I have never been one to give a damn what someone says or thinks of me, but I am married and have a career to think about. I couldn't let something like that ruin me. Besides, to me I felt it was just a phase. I've never been into women. And to this day, I never desired to be with women like that at all."

A half-smile came across Nadine's face as she thought about a time she and the mystery woman had shared. Nadine ever revealed who the woman was because she had promised her that she would never tell anyone her name or anything personal about her. Cheryl was glad to see her smiling but was also curious as to what was making her smile.

"I'm glad to see you smile again. What are you thinking about?"

"Talking about her just brings back so many good memories. I mean, besides the fling, she was a great listener and friend." Both women giggled at the way Nadine spoke about how good the memories were.

"I mean, it's normal that you got attached to her. She's a female, and we understand each other better than a man ever will. We all have that emotional bond," Cheryl said. They sat there for at least another hour or so and talked about Nadine's freaky affair with the woman. Neither of them realized how late it was getting until Nadine's phone rang. It was her husband. She wanted so badly to pick up, but she decided against it. It caught Cheryl's attention, and she looked down at her watch and knew she had to go and get the kids from her aunts.

"Oh wow, look at the time! I hate to have to wrap this up, but I have to go and get my kids and handle a few things."

"That's fine. I actually need to be leaving myself."

"Before you go, I want to suggest something to you. You can try it if you want. If you really want to be with your husband and want to put all this in the past, I want you to try sitting him down and talking it over with him. Don't force anything on him or try and make him come to counseling. When he is ready, he will come around. Now, since you say he is normally away and communicating over the phone rarely works, start writing him letters. Each time he goes away, send him a letter expressing your feelings," Cheryl said, handing her a journal that included a pen.

Nadine really didn't see how this would work, but she was willing to try anything to save her marriage. "Are you sure this is going to work?" Nadine asked Cheryl with a puzzled looked on her face.

"You can never be sure if something is going to work. You just have to take the risk and fight for what you want and love. This is just something I want you and him to try in order to help you guys communicate better. Tell him your feelings and express yourself in your writing. Give him a chance to express what he's feeling as well."

"It seems a bit childish and weird to me, but I am open to anything that will help save my marriage," Nadine said as she began to fidget with the journal.

Cheryl understood that it might seem a bit middle-school to be writing letters and notes, but she really felt that this would help Nadine cope with what she and her husband were going through. "I can understand that it seems a bit childish, but because you said that you have a hard time communicating with each other, I just figured this could be a way you can communicate and avoid the arguing and things like that. Another reason I feel this writing will be good thing for you is because you said you never get a chance to express your feelings and you don't have many friends. So now you can write down your emotions and how you are feeling."

Nadine took a moment to think about what she had said, and it seemed to be much clearer to her. She was beginning to understand the logic behind this whole writing exercise. She glanced down at the journal and took a deep breath. She knew she could fill the whole book; there was so much she held inside, things that she hadn't even told Cheryl and didn't think that she would or could. Nadine knew there were unanswered questions she had to ask her husband, and now that this was brought to her attention, she would use it to her advantage and ask him all the things she had been afraid to ask.

"I really see what you mean about this writing. I just had to sit here and think about all the things I hold inside that bother me." Nadine let out a little chuckle. "Although, I think that you might have to give me like six more of these with all the things I have inside." They both laughed at Nadine's joke.

"It's good to see you have a good sense of humor about this. Most people become negative and feel that it is a waste of time. I can totally understand why, but that's why I am just here to voice my opinion, and if it is something you decide to go with, I will be here to help you. Just remember that I cannot make all the choices for you with your marriage. You are going to have to take charge as well."

"I totally understand where you are coming from, and I appreciate your help. I really hope that this works, and if not, then it is not meant to be," Nadine said, fidgeting with her hands again. She seemed nervous after she made the last statement, and Cheryl could tell. Since it was getting a little late, and Cheryl was ready to go home and deal with her own issues, she decided to end the session. She and Nadine said a few more words and then scheduled another meeting for next Friday to check her progress with her husband. Nadine agreed, left, and headed home.

Cheryl stayed in the office for about another hour or so to go over some notes from sessions she had had earlier in the week and to check on the progress of her website. Things were going pretty smoothly with her new accomplishments, and in a few weeks, her site would be up and running, and she would have a whole new line of clients. Cheryl smiled at her accomplishments. The smile quickly turned into a frown as she looked at the picture of her and her husband that hung high on her wall. All she could do was shake her head at the thought of what he was doing to her, after all she had done for him. She was the one who really got him all clean and legal, and this was the thanks she got!

"I can't believe this bitch has the nerve to be stepping out on me, and I have been nothing but faithful to his ass!" She buried her face in her hands, and tears formed in her eyes she tried hard to make since of this whole thing. But nothing really made sense. After sitting and daydreaming for about ten minutes, she gathered her things and headed out the door. As soon as she walked up to her truck, her phone rang. It was him; she really didn't want to answer, and although she had said and thought of all the things she would do or say to him, she was just too tired to get into any of it. Instead of answering it, she pressed the end button and sent it to voicemail. She knew he would call back, so she decided to turn the phone completely off. During the drive home, she had nothing but complete silence, and it gave her time to think about what she was going to do. The thought of leaving him was crazy. She was so in love with her husband, and she couldn't understand why he would want to do something like this to her. In all her years of helping other women (and even men) and giving advice, this was the one time she really didn't know what to say or do. It was a fucked up situation she was in, and she just wanted it all to be over. She didn't want to be around him any longer, and she needed some time to just think. So she made a note to plan a getaway for herself and her girls, Keyshia and Joy. Cheryl knew that Joy could use a vacation with all that she was going through with the divorce, and she knew Keyshia would be down to go anywhere with liquor, partying, and men. As she reached her driveway, she noticed a few lights on. That meant he was up waiting for her to get there. She took a deep breath and got out of her truck. She didn't want to argue or fight with him, so she decided to go in at peace. As soon as she entered the door, she saw him sitting on the couch watching television. She pretended that she didn't notice him, walked right past him, and headed upstairs. She put her things down and headed to the kids' room to give them a kiss. They were sleeping so peacefully. The sight of how handsome they were made her want to cry and made her wonder why in the world he would want to lose anything as precious as this. Many men would kill to have the life that he was living, and here he was fucking it up for a piece of pussy. The dumb shit men do just to catch a fucking nut! As she headed back to her bedroom, she noticed that he was just standing in the hall staring at her. Instead of saying anything to him, she walked right past him and went to the room to gather her things to take a shower.

Chuck was getting pissed that Cheryl was ignoring him and not saying anything to him. He didn't know what to say and really didn't know how much she knew. He decided to walk in the room behind her to see exactly what she knew and what was wrong with her.

"Hey, sweetheart, what's going on? I can't get a hug a kiss or anything? I mean, damn…"

Before he could say another word, Cheryl snapped, "What the fuck? Are you serious? You know damn well that you don't deserve a fucking hug, kiss, or shit. Nigga, please. Don't be coming to me like you don't know what the fuck's wrong with me. Look, I ain't in the mood for this bullshit with you, and my fucking kids are in the other room asleep, so leave me the fuck alone. Let me take a shower, so I can rest my nerves." She walked into the bathroom, leaving Chuck shocked. He had never heard Cheryl go off the way she just did. He was stuck and didn't know what to do. He couldn't come out and just tell her what had been going on, but he felt bad that he was hurting her and his family. He sat on the bed with his head buried in his hands. About an hour later, Cheryl came out of the shower, did her nightly routine, and massaged her legs in Victoria's Secret Plum Drop lotion. She smelled delicious.

Chuck knew that she was the forbidden fruit, and he dared not to touch. She walked right past him, took her blanket and pillow, and headed to the guest bedroom, leaving him sitting on the edge of the bed looking like a dumbass. Chuck's feelings were hurt even more. He knew that he had fucked up and that it was going to take a lot to make things right if he wanted to save his marriage and family. He thought about going after her, but he knew it was too late to be arguing, and the kids were sleeping. So instead, he just lay back on the bed and tried to fall asleep. In the meantime, Cheryl was in the guestroom down the hall, crying her eyeballs out. She cried until she fell asleep.

Chapter Five

THE NEXT MORNING WHEN CHERYL finally got up, she freshened up and went to the kids' room to get them up. She was surprised when she went to their room and saw that they were not there. She headed downstairs and noticed that no one was in the house. She glanced over at the clock and noticed that it was a quarter to twelve. "Oh shit, I've been sleep all that time, and this asshole didn't even have the decency to wake me up. Ugh, he is really starting to get under my fucking skin!" she yelled, grabbing the cordless phone to call him to give him a piece of her mind. As soon as she began to dial his number, she heard the door open, and she knew it was him. She slammed the phone down and stormed into the living room. Once she noticed that the kids were not with him, she went off.

"Why in the fuck would you allow me to sleep that long? What if I had to meet a client or something? You know damn well I do not stay in bed that long. You are really starting to piss me the fuck off with your bullshit. And where are my fucking kids?" She was on a roll; you could see the sweat forming around her nose and her nostrils flaring. Chuck stood there in a daze. He didn't know what to do or say. He thought for a moment that she was the devil standing in front of him. He wanted to shake her hard, so his wife could come back, but then again he was a bit sick of hearing her talk shit to him like he was not her husband.

"Look, I don't know what the hell your problem is, but I'm sick of you talking to me like I'm a fucking child. I know you didn't have any meetings or anything today; that's why I let your ass sleep since you've been walking around here with your ass on your shoulders. I thought I would let you get some rest. And as far as our kids are concerned, they are fine. They're with their grandparents. Don't you remember they said they wanted to get them to take them to that new water park? Or were you so busy being pissed off at the world that you forgot?" Chuck said in a firm and angry tone. He somewhat had a clue what she was mad about, but instead of admitting to anything just yet, he had decided to play along and lie as long as he could until he was able to straighten things out.

But Cheryl couldn't believe her ears. He was standing there trying to flip this on her, but what he didn't know was that he was really about to feel her wrath. "You've got some fucking nerves coming in here trying to flip this all on me. Nigga, you know good and damn well why I'm pissed off, but you're going to sit up here and play fucking dumb. News flash, bitch, if you want to play these fucking games, I will play them right along with your ass. You mark my fucking words when I say that I will be the bitch with the last laugh," Cheryl said as she began to walk out the room.

Instead of letting her go, Chuck grabbed her by the arm. She tried to yank away, but he had a grip on her. Chuck's holding her only made matters worse, and the next thing you know, she reached for the first thing she saw to hit him with. She grabbed the vase that was sitting on the end table and busted the shit out of his head. She had hit him so hard that he had no choice but to let her go and grab his head. The blood began to stream down his head onto his face. He tired wiping it with his hand, but it began to flow heavier. They were shocked that she had hit him because they had never, in all the years of their, marriage had any violent arguments. Cheryl was nervous, and seeing the blood shook her even more. She didn't know what to do, and Chuck was losing so much blood at this point. The next thing she knew, he had passed out. Cheryl screamed at the top of her lungs as she saw him fall to the floor. Everything in her went numb. She shook herself out of it and called the ambulance. When they arrived, she told them she heard a noise in the living room, and when she came to see what it was, she saw Chuck lying on the floor and she called 9-1-1. They rushed him to the hospital, and the whole time, all Cheryl could do was cry.

A part of her thought, *that's good for his ass,* but the sincere part hoped and prayed that he would be alright. The doctors and officers asked a few more questions before they went to find out his status, so she could be able to see him. On the way over, Cheryl had called Joy to come to the hospital to sit with her. As she sat in the waiting area, Joy and Keyshia came running in, opening their arms to embrace their friend. Tears ran down her cheeks as they both held her tight. They didn't know what had happened. Cheryl had just called Joy crying, saying that she was at the hospital with Chuck and to come sit with her. A few moments later, they sat her down and gave her some tissue to clean her face.

"Cher, what happened to Chuck? Where are the kids? Are they alright?" Joy began to panic. Keyshia was so nervous that she didn't know what to say. They both wanted answers and waited for Cheryl to catch her breath, so they could find out what had happened. Cheryl wiped her eyes and looked up at them both. She saw the worry in their eyes, and she didn't want them to worry so much.

"No, the kids are fine. They're with their grandparents," she said. Then she paused and put her head down. She really didn't want to tell them the truth either, but they had always been there for her no matter what, so she couldn't tell them a lie. "Chuck and I got into an argument, and I hit him in the head with a vase, and he passed out."

Before she could finish, Keyshia burst out into laughter. Joy nudged Keyshia in her side for being so rude. Keyshia didn't respond because she knew exactly why Joy did it. So instead of responding to the nudge, she wiped the smirk off her face because she knew it had to be something serious for Cheryl to have hit Chuck. Cheryl didn't mind the fact that Keyshia laughed; she wanted to laugh herself, but she was too afraid and nervous. She didn't know what to think, and she was scared she may have seriously hurt her husband, the father of her kids. Cheryl was sitting in silence, hoping that they would just drop it and not ask her any questions about the whole situation. But that wish would not be granted today. Joy broke the silence because she really wanted to know what was going on, and she was determined to get some answers.

"Cher, I know that you may not be in the mood to discuss this, but I'm worried, and I need to know what is really up with you and Chuck. I mean, I know that no relationship is perfect, and everyone has disagreements and stuff, but this is not like you guys. Is it that serious you had to bust this nigga in his shit?"

Cheryl let out a long sigh. Anyone could tell by her body language that she was a bit annoyed and wasn't in the mood for this, but she knew that her friends would not let it go, so she decided to tell them. "Yes, Joy, it's that serious—real serious for that matter. Remember I told y'all I saw this nigga car at the fucking motel on Biscayne? Well, once again Mr. Chuck was out giving his dick to some bitch other than his wife, and he had the audacity to come home and pretend that shit was all peaches and cream."

They both looked at her with a surprised look on their faces. Neither of them could say a word. They remembered her telling them, but they never thought that Cheryl and Chuck would have any adultery issues. They were the ideal couple in everyone's eyes, so to hear that Chuck was really cheating was very shocking. Cheryl could tell by the look on Joy's and Keyshia's faces that they were surprised, and it kind of pissed her off a little. She knew that they were like all the other people who felt that since she was a therapist and she and Chuck seemed happy on the outside, they wouldn't have any problems like any other normal couple would. She couldn't understand why people always judged a book by the cover and made their own interpretations without even knowing the whole story.

"Yeah, y'all shocked, huh? Thought it was impossible for this to happen to me, huh? I thought the same thing, and that was the biggest mistake that I ever made. I should have known better and seen this coming. How could I have been so damn stupid and blind?"

Joy and Keyshia really didn't know what to say. They wouldn't say they thought Cher's marriage was perfect; they just didn't expect anything like this.

"Cher, you're not stupid. Don't say that! You can't beat yourself up about this. You had no clue this would happen. You have always told me to never blame myself for things I did not do, so there is no need to blame yourself," Joy stated as she rubbed Cheryl's back.

"Joy is right. You are a wonderful person, mother, and wife. No one really expects these types of things to happen to them. You just have to be strong," Keyshia said.

Cheryl really didn't know what to do next. She loved her husband without a doubt, and she really didn't want to take the kids through a divorce. She needed some time to think about her next move, to breathe, and to take this all in. To her, the cheating part was not what hurt the most. It was the fact that she knew the other woman. She couldn't seem to understand how Chuck or this chick could try her like this.

Cheryl wiped her tears and told her girls that she was going to go to the restroom and freshen up before the doctor come back. They both said that they would go. As soon as they got up to go with her, the doctor came out of the room to talk to Cheryl. As he walked towards her, she could feel her knees get weak. She was so nervous, and she didn't know what to expect. They had been in the hospital for a few hours, and she was afraid that they were going to tell her that Chuck was dead. She didn't know she had enough power to knock him unconscious for this long.

"Mrs. Michaels, I have some good news. Chuck is finally conscious. He may be a bit groggy, but you can go in and see him in a bit. I do want to ask you what actually happened. The examination has shown that Chuck was hit with a heavy object using blunt force. Is there something else that happened that you want to tell me about?"

Cheryl didn't know what to say, and she was afraid that he would call the police or some shit. But with the way she was feeling, she just wanted to get this day over with, so she thought, *Fuck it.*

"Well to be honest, Dr. Martin..." She took a deep breath and continued, "Chuck and I got into a heated argument, and the next thing I knew, I had busted him cross the head. I won't stand here and say I didn't mean to hit him because I very much wanted to knock his ass out, but I didn't expect it to go this far."

"I totally understand. This is nothing out of the norm. I have seen married couples go through worse. The good thing about this is that you came out of it without a scratch. You are one of the lucky ones, and thank God for that. Now I can't say that I condone what you did and that violence is the answer, but you have to protect yourself. There are also other ways to resolve things without violence. I will keep this between us and not report it."

Cheryl thanked Dr. Martin, and they chatted a little more. Then she went and told Joy and Keyshia that she was about to go in and see Chuck and asked if they were going to wait. They both said they had a few things to get done and told her to call them as soon as she left the hospital. They hugged each other and said their goodbyes.

Then Cheryl headed towards Chuck's room. Cheryl was afraid and nervous as she walked into Chuck's room. As she entered, she found him sitting up in the bed watching TV. She eased into the room and closed the door. She slowly made her way over to the chair next to his bed. Before she could sit down, he looked up at her and yelled, "What the fuck just happened to me?" He looked at Cheryl with an angry and confused look on his face, as if this should have happened to anybody else but him.

She stood there shocked, not knowing what to do or say. Part of her wanted to curse his ass out, slap the shit out of him, and leave. She knew she couldn't act up in the hospital, but after what Chuck yelled out, she was ready to give it to his ass. Before she could utter a word, he yelled out again. "I said what the fuck just happened to me! You're standing there looking all crazy and shit, but your fucking mouth ain't moving."

Before he could finish, Cheryl lost it. "Motherfucker, you better be glad your ass is still breathing. Nigga, you got me fucked up. You've got the nerve to be sitting up here, demanding me to tell you what happened. How about you tell me what the fuck happened to us? Nigga, you got me all fucked up. You're the one who has some explaining to do. You call yourself trying to beat me getting mad. Man, please find some other lame bitch to play with." Cheryl took a deep breath. She could see that she was getting a bit loud, and that was way out of her character.

"Look I'm not about to sit up here and argue and go through this shit with you. I'm pretty sure you know why I busted you in your shit and you ended up here. So we are not going to play this game. I just wanted to make sure you were alive for the kids' sake. I'm not with this shit right now. I'm about to go, so I advise you to either call your other bitch or somebody else to come get your stank ass when they're ready to let you leave."

Cheryl grabbed her purse and headed for the door, but Chuck told her to wait. Deep down inside, he knew that she was pissed at him and that he was wrong, so he deserved to hear everything she was saying to him. But never in a million years would he have imagined that she would do something like this to him. He didn't know exactly what to say to her, but he didn't want her to leave just yet.

"Cheryl, wait. So you're seriously going to just leave me here? We need to talk about this, and if anybody knows that we can't just avoid this, it's you."

She cut him off again. She really didn't want to hear shit he had to say at this moment because not once did he say sorry or anything. All he was worried about was his fucking self, and she really didn't care to hear that shit.

"Chuck, I've already said what I had to say. I'm not in the mood to deal with this shit. Yeah, I know we need to talk, but this is neither the time nor place. The least you can do is respect my mind and let me leave in peace. We can deal with this later on. And oh yes, I will be leaving your black ass right here, and I will not be back."

Cheryl walked out of the room and headed to the elevator, leaving Chuck looking stupid in the face. Chuck knew he was wrong, and he had no choice but to let her leave, even though he didn't want to. For the next ten minutes, Chuck sat up in bed thinking about the event that had taken place. He wondered how much Cheryl had actually seen. Part of him knew that she could have not seen much because she really didn't say much, but then again she could just be trying to avoid it. He was so nervous and scared. He knew what he was doing was wrong, and he didn't want to lose his family and everything they had built together. He knew he was going to have to seriously end this affair no matter what.

For the next few days, Cheryl spent time with the kids. She took a few days off and cancelled most of her appointments. Chuck was due to come home from the hospital today, so she decided to take the kids over to her mom's. She didn't want them to have to see any tension between her and Chuck. It was bad enough that she had told them that their father was sick and had to go to the hospital. She wanted them to see him, but she needed to get a few things off her chest first.

Cheryl was sitting in her home office going over some paperwork and information for the online clients she was soon to take on. Cheryl had decided that since she enjoyed what she did, she wanted to take an advice column to a whole new level. She wanted to be able to have virtual clientele. She had never known any marriage counselors and therapists who had extended their expertise virtually, and this was something she wanted to do. Her site and everything was scheduled to be completed by next month. There were a few things she had to get in order and a lot of advertising she needed to get done. She really wanted to focus on two major states for the time being. Her home-state of Florida would be her main state, and she was kind of torn on what would be the other state. Whatever state she decided on, she planned on going to visit so that she could advertise as well as meet a few other people because she was also looking to expand her offices. Her practice was doing well. She had started out with only three clients, and that included her friend Joy. Now, about five years later, she had well over fifteen clients and was gaining more and more each day. So it was kind of hard to keep up with appointments and things like that.

Cheryl was in deep thought and going through some paperwork when she heard the door close. Her office was not too far from the living room, so she could hear Chuck come in. She took a deep breath and got ready for whatever was coming. She stayed at her desk and continued to work. It took a while before Chuck realized she was in her office, and he walked in and sat on her sofa. For the first few moments, they sat in silence and didn't say a word to each other. Chuck got restless and decided to speak first, being that the situation they were in was his fault.

"Cheryl, look. I'm sorry. I don't really know what to say that can change any of this, but I know that I want you, and I want our family to stay together."

Cheryl didn't respond; she really didn't know how to. Being home alone had given her time to think the situation over, and as much as she wanted to fuck Chuck and this chick up, she had decided against it. See, Cheryl always worried about her appearance more than anything, so she never wanted to have anyone see her going through anything. That was just the type of person she was; she always smiled through any pain she had and made the best out of bad situations. So she had decided to end this bullshit with Chuck before it got out to the public.

"Look, Chuck. I had time to think about all this shit, and I really don't want to do this. I can't go through this shit with you right now. I have a lot that is going on for me and my practice right now, and I have people that I need to help. So I'm only going to say this once: Leave the bitch alone, and I fucking mean it. I don't want people in my fucking business, and going through a divorce right now would be too much for my career and the kids. So take this warning and know that if I ever fucking catch your ass again, or if I even fucking think you may be trying me, I'm going to take my .45 and put a fucking hole in you and that bitch. If you don't believe me, try me and see."

Chuck was shocked, and when he looked into her eyes, he could see flames. He never knew his wife could be so evil, but he knew by the tone in her voice and the look in her eyes that she was not bullshitting. He didn't want to have to find out if she was bluffing or not, so he decided that he was going to end his li'l thing he had going on.

"I understand, Cher. Baby, I'm truly sorry. I know it's going to take some time for us to get over this, and I want you to know that I will do anything in my power to make this right."

"Chuck, honestly, save all that shit right now. I'm only doing this for the sake of the kids and my career. I love you and all, but how you did me is fucked up."

Chuck felt bad because he knew that he had hurt her, and he could tell it was killing her to even be in his presence. Before he could say anything else, Cheryl said, "Look, I need some time away from all this. I'm too stressed to be in this environment. I'm going to take a few days off and go on a mini-vacation. You are welcome to go and get the kids from my mom's house, or you can leave them there until I get back."

"When are you leaving, and where are you going?"

"All that is not really important. You will know when I leave. As for now, the guestroom is fixed up to your liking. You can get yourself comfortable there until I leave. If you decide to go get the kids, you can sleep in the master once until I leave. I'd prefer they not know about our problems or have to ask any questions right now."

Chuck was speechless. He knew she was mad, but damn, this was a bit extreme. He didn't even know how to respond to her. Instead, he nodded his head and let her know he understood, and she was satisfied with that. He got up, left her office, and headed upstairs to take a shower. Meanwhile, Cheryl didn't think any more of it. Instead, she got to work and left the rest of the evening quiet.

Chapter Six

As Chuck entered the guest room, he saw a few of his things in there. Cheryl wasn't playing when she said she had set it up to his likings. Chuck plopped down on the bed and just sat there in silence. He thought about what he had done and knew he had to end this li'l phase he was going through. There was no doubt that he loved his wife and kids. Just the thought of losing them scared him shitless, and he didn't understand how he had gotten himself caught up in what he was doing. Chuck knew he was dead wrong on so many levels, because Cher had never given him a reason to try her the way he did.

Damn, I fucked up! Chuck thought to himself. Then he wondered how much she really knew. *She couldn't know much 'cause I doubt she would've let me live.*

He let out a long sigh. Part of him was scared, but another part was a bit at ease because he doubted that she really knew everything. He knew he really had to end this shit before she found out anything else. Although he was in deep, he loved his wife and family way more than this little thing he had going on. Chuck sat and thought a little while longer. Then he took a shower and went to see the kids. Cheryl went with him, but on the ride there, she was silent. Once they got there and saw the kids, the kids asked to come home.

"Mommy, can we come home with you and daddy?" the kids asked.

Cheryl didn't want to let them come because she didn't want Chuck in the same room as her, but she couldn't say no to such adorable faces. Once they got home and the kids were taking a bath, she walked over to Chuck and said, "You can stay downstairs and watch TV until the kids fall asleep. I don't want them to see you going in the guestroom to sleep."

Then she walked off to go check on the kids. Chuck had a look on his face that said, "What the hell?" He thought that since they were laughing and stuff with the kids, he would be able to sleep in their bedroom, but to his surprise, she was not having that shit. So he did what he was told and left the night like that.

For the rest of the week, things were very tense at home between them. Cheryl was sick of walking on eggshells. She hated being away from her kids, but she needed the time away. So that Saturday morning she stayed in her home office, went over some work, and contacted a few business people to set up some meetings. She planned on having some fun, but she was always about her money. She first had to decide on a place. Since she and Joy hadn't really talked since all this shit had been going on, she decided to call her to tell her the plans.

"Hey, boo! What's good?" Joy said in a high-pitched, perky voice.

"Nothing much. I miss you. Sorry I've been so distant these past few days," Cheryl responded.

"I miss you, too, and you know I understand. Besides, your ass used to do that a lot back in the day," Joy said, laughing.

"Do what back in the day?" Cheryl asked as she laughed.

"Yeah, you better laugh 'cause you know exactly what I'm talking about. Every time you went through something or whatever, you would shut people out and go missing. That shit used to piss me off, but I understood," Joy said in a sarcastic tone.

"Look, let's not even go there today. You and Keyshia love bringing up the past and stuff," Cheryl said.

"Bitch, that's 'cause we've got history, and we've had some times together. Damn, how time flies!" Joy said. She let out a sigh as she thought back on all the shit they had done and been through. They were both silent for a moment as their thoughts drifted back in time.

Cheryl snapped out of it first. "Yes, we did have some good times. Those were the good ol' days. But time must go on, and we can still have fun like that. That's why I called you."

Before Cheryl could finish, Joy interrupted her. "Oh, really? What kind of fun are you talking bout cause you know how you can act at times? You never really want to go anywhere. It's all about work, work, work!"

Cheryl had figured joy would have some slick shit to say, but what she said was a bit true. She hated that her friend was right. She wondered, *Damn, have I really gotten that boring? Maybe that's why this asshole fucked around on me.* She quickly turned off those thoughts, so she wouldn't get pissed off 'cause she really wasn't in the mood to deal with this shit.

"Whatever! I can't help the fact that I am busy with work, but I still make time to chill with y'all sometimes."

"Yeah, you can say that again… Sometimes!" They both laughed. "But naw, on a serious note, I need a damn vacation. There's too much going on, and I need some time away from this shit. So I figured you could use one too, and well, Keyshia… You know that chick's down for whatever," Cheryl said.

"Okay, cool. Sounds good. And you're right. I do need a damn getaway cause I'm 'bout sick of Miami and all this bullshit. So when are we leaving, and where we going? Wait—before you answer that, this is going to be a vacation for us to have fun and just get away from all this bullshit for a while, right? And not for one of your business trips? 'cause I know how you do," Joy said and then got silent to wait to see what Cheryl was going to say.

Cheryl began to chuckle before she decided to respond because her friend knew her to well.

"Cher, don't play with me! What the hell are you laughing for? That shit there is not funny. I figured it was too good to be true with your ass."

"Joy, stop acting all dramatic and shit. It ain't even like that. I really need a damn vacation, but at the same time, you know I'm 'bout my money."

"Yeah, bitch, we all 'bout our money, but shit! Live a little!" Joy understood Cheryl, but it did sometimes piss her off that her friend never really enjoyed life the way she thought she should.

"Bitch, listen. I do enjoy life. Just 'cause I don't club all the time doesn't mean I don't have fun. I'm older. I did all that shit when we were younger."

"Child, we are not all that old. I'm not saying go clubbing, but shit, do something, bitch," Joy said, and they both laughed.

"On the real, let's not get into this right now. Just let's pick a place 'cause I'm undecided on either New York or Cali."

"Oooh, bitch, let's go to Cali! I've always wanted to go there!" Joy practically screamed through the phone. You could hear the excitement in her voice. She sounded like a big kid on Christmas. Cheryl couldn't do anything but laugh at how Joy was yelling through the phone.

"Dang, chick! Calm down. You sound worse than the kids," Cheryl said, laughing. After Joy finally calmed down Cheryl gave her girl a few of the details of their trip and told her to call Keyshia and fill her in. They planned on meeting later that night to go over their plans. Cheryl wanted to surprise them. She was going to pay for the whole trip for both of her girls, but she decided to tell them when she saw them together that night.

After hanging up with Cheryl, Joy was headed to take a shower. Before she could get in the bathroom, her cell phone rang. She was hesitant about answering it, but she didn't know if it was an emergency. So she grabbed her robe and headed for her phone in the bedroom. When she reached her phone, she didn't recognize the number. *Ugh, who in the fuck is this?* she thought to herself. Instead of answering it, she placed it back on the bed and walked away. As soon as she got to the door, it started ringing again. Joy turned around and went to answer it.

"Who is this?"

For a moment, the person on the other end didn't say anything. Joy waited to see if the person on the other end would finally say something. Instead, the person hung up; that pissed her off.

"What the fuck?" she said as she looked down at her phone. She didn't think much more of it because she had something to do. As soon as she walked off, it rang again. This time, she just let it ring and went to take her shower. When she finished her shower and began to get dressed, she grabbed her phone and saw that she had thirteen missed calls. Out of all the calls, eleven of the calls were from the number that had called her before she went to take a shower, and two calls were from her aunt. She was a bit pissed and curious to know who this person was. So she called the number, but there was no answer. She called back again, and this time a woman answered.

"Hello! Who is this?" Joy asked as soon as the person answered the phone.

"You called me, so who is this?" the voice on the other end said.

Joy was ready to go off, but she wanted to know who in the hell this chick was.

"Look, I had not one but eleven missed calls from this number. So I'm calling back to see who in the hell is this!" Joy really wasn't in the mood because she had other things to do.

"Look, I called by mistake, so don't worry about it."

That just pissed Joy off even more. She was wondering what in the hell was going on. "How in the hell do you make a mistake over ten times and call the same damn number? Please, tell me, how is that possible?"

Instead of answering Joy, the chick on the other end of the phone hung up. That shit sent chills up Joy's body. She was beyond pissed. "Who the fuck is this bitch, and why in the fuck is she trying me?" Joy was heated. She attempted to call the bitch back, but right before she could press call, her phone started to ring. She didn't even pay attention to see who it was; she just answered.

"Look, bitch, if you've got something to say, state your fucking name and problem, and stop playing on my damn phone!" Joy yelled in the phone because she thought it was the same chick calling her back. To her surprise, it was her aunt.

"Joy, what is your damn problem talking to me like that? What the fuck you got going on?" Tracy said in an angry and confused tone. Tracy was Joy's aunt who always called when she needed or wanted help. Joy always found herself helping or giving her money because she had been there for her in the past, but lately she had been ignoring her. Her favors had long ago run out. Joy noticed the only reason and time Tracy would call was when she needed or wanted something, so she had been dodging and ignoring all her calls. Now to slip up and answer Tracy had only made her madder.

Damn, why the fuck did I have to answer for this lady? My ass should have been paying attention, Joy thought to herself. She took a deep breath to prepare herself to deal with Tracy and her bullshit.

"Hey. Sorry 'bout that. Somebody's playing on my damn phone, and I didn't even look to see who was calling before I answered. But my bad. What's up?" Joy said in a real dry tone.

"Why the hell is somebody playing on your phone?"

"The hell if I know, but that shit's got me pissed."

"Well, just calm down. If they really want to talk, they will. Or just don't answer," Tracy told her.

Joy could hear in her aunt's voice that she wasn't interested in hearing about Joy's li'l issue. She could tell she was just ready to get to why she called.

"Ugh, yeah. I hear you. But what's up, Auntie?"

"I was just calling to see how you've been and how the divorce coming is along," Tracy said while rolling her eyes. She really wasn't interested in Joy's problem. She was calling because she wanted some money.

Joy already knew that, and this time she planned on telling Tracy no. She was sick of her family damn-near sucking her dry and bugging her with their problems. So all that shit Tracy was talking about just calling to see how she was a lie. "I'm doing well. Everything is just fine. "

"That's good to hear. You sound like you're doing better. I told you God will work everything out," Tracy told her.

"Well, you're right. Hey auntie, I was headed to a meeting. I need to finish getting ready. I don't mean to rush off the phone, but I'm going to have to call you later." Joy was trying to rush her aunt off the phone.

"Oh, okay, but before you go, I need a favor," Tracy said.

"What favor, Aunt Tracy?" Joy said in a dry tone.

"Well, I've got some bills I need to catch up on, and I need to borrow like $700. I will…"

Joy was pissed, so she cut Tracy off before she could finish. "Aunt Tracy, I don't have that kind of money. Why do y'all always call asking for damn favors? Damn, y'all see I'm going through a divorce, and you would think y'all would be more considerate. I can't help you this time. I'm sorry."

"What you mean y'all, and somebody's always calling asking you for shit? Girl, you must not remember all the help I've given you and this family!" Tracy always pulled that card. Normally Joy would fall for it and feel guilty and give her aunt or any other family member what they asked for, but the bank had finally closed.

"Listen, Bank of Joy is officially fucking closed. I'm sick of y'all calling me asking me for shit and always being quick to say what you've done for me. For the record, y'all haven't done shit for me, and as far as the little you claim to have done, I've paid my debt. Damn, when is someone going to do something for fucking Joy? I've got my own shit to worry about, and I'm sick of taking care of everybody else. So if you don't like it, oh well! I still love you, but I'm done," Joy told her aunt in a very rude and agitated tone.

Tracy was shocked at how Joy was talking to her. It had her speechless, and she sat silently on the phone for a moment. Then she rolled her eyes and said, "I don't know who you're talking to. Obviously you've got some issues, so I'mma give you time to cool the fuck off 'cause…"

Before she could finish, Joy cut her off. This time, it wasn't pleasant at all. "Fuck you and all that shit you're talking, Tracy. Call me when you can do something for me. In the meantime, talk to the silence once I hang up!" Joy hung up her phone and threw it on the bed. She was pissed—the nerve of her aunt! "This bitch has really got some nerves calling me with this bullshit. Damn, I'm sick of them!" Joy yelled as she sat on the bed.

Her family was always calling her for favors and had been asking for money for years, and she took care of them, but enough was enough. They were all grown, but they decided to make different choices in life. Joy normally felt bad and felt that she was obligated to help, but everyone always tried to tell her to stop taking care of them. She never listened, but now she was getting sick of it, so it was time to cut them loose. That was that! Joy took a deep breath and relaxed her mind. Then she got up and headed where she needed to handle her business for the day.

Later on that night, Joy and Keyshia met Cheryl to have drinks and to discuss the trip. Cheryl had gotten there a little late because she had an argument with Chuck. He kept saying he was sick of the way things were, but she really didn't give a fuck how he felt. When she arrived, Keyshia and Joy were already seated. She got to the table and greeted her friends. "Hey, babes! Sorry I'm a little late," Cheryl said before she took her seat.

"It's cool. We not too long ago got here ourselves," Joy replied.

"So what's good, boo?" Keyshia said in an excited tone. She was always ready to party. "I hear that we're going on a vacation. You know I can't wait. New state and city with new dudes!" Keyshia said, and they all burst into laughter. Keyshia was sipping on her drink and bouncing in the seat. She was ready.

"Girl, you're a damn fool. That's why I love having you around," Cheryl said and chuckled.

"Of course both of y'all bitches love having Keyshia around; she's is the life of the party!" Keyshia said referring to herself. They began to laugh again at her response. They always had fun, no matter what, as long as they were together.

"So what's this surprise you have for us?" Joy asked in a childlike voice.

"Well, it's nothing major," Cheryl replied.

"What do you mean nothing major? Shit, I thought we were 'bout to get a new car or something," Keyshia said jokingly, and that really made them laugh.

"Girl, you're something else. No, I'm not buying you bitches a damn car or anything like that. But because I love y'all and really want and need a getaway, I'm paying for the whole trip to LA. Everything…"

Before she could finish, Keyshia and Joy were screaming and yelling. "Are you fucking serious? Oh my god, oh my god! You are the best!" They were extremely happy about what Cheryl shared with them.

So for the next hour or so, the girls had a few more drinks and chatted a bit more. They went over more details about what they would do on the trip. The ladies said their goodbyes at the end of the night and planned on leaving the next week. They would be gone for a week and three days. Over the next few days, they all handled their business with work and home and arranged things for when they were away on the trip. On that Sunday, they caught their flight. It was goodbye, Miami, and hello, Los Angeles! Once they arrived at the airport in LA, everything felt so clean, fresh, and different.

"Ah, now this is the life!" Joy said as she took a deep breath to take in the fresh air.

"Yes! Oh my god! It feels so good to be in a different environment. I can't wait to enjoy this. So let's stop standing here, bitches. Let's get to it!" Keyshia said and started skipping out the door. The ladies picked up their car from the rental company and then headed to the hotel. The suite they had was incredible, and the view was breathtaking. It was a three-bedroom, three-bathroom suite that sat right on the beach. It had a huge kitchen with a separate dining and living room. It was amazing. They could not believe their eyes; Cheryl had outdone herself.

"Damn, Cheryl, this is so fucking amazing. Thank you, thank you! You're the best!" Joy said and gave her a hug. Keyshia was speechless, pretty much gasping for air. Everything was lovely. They got settled and decided to stay in for the rest of their night. Besides, Cheryl had an early meeting the next morning. She was meeting up with the people she was hiring to market her website and to help her find other successful therapists in her field who would be willing to work with her. So they sat out on the balcony, and sipped some wine, and chatted.

The next morning, Cheryl got up to head to her meeting. Keyshia and Joy decided to just lie back and relax until she got back. Cheryl met up with her people, and they discussed how everything would go. Her website would be launched in two weeks. Cheryl wanted it to be a place where people could feel comfortable opening up to her. The strategy was to provide responses to people within forty-eight hours of the post. People could become members, and there would be a small fee of $25 per month. She would also have virtual sessions twice a week, and each session would be forty-five minutes long. Clients who would select that option would pay $40 per session. Now Cheryl didn't want to overwhelm herself as she knew that she couldn't help everyone, and that's where the people she was meeting came into play.

"Okay, guys. Here is what I really want to do. You know I will have the virtual session as well as respond to questions. Now, being that I still have my regular clientele back in Miami, I'm going to need a few more people to work the site with me."

Cheryl's accountant was in the meeting as well and was trying to make sure she was really doing the right thing. "Now, Cheryl, we will have to go over numbers and other important matters before deciding to add more people to the payroll. I think you should at least wait two months or so to see how it starts out. You don't want to add too many people to the payroll and then not bring in enough profit from this venture to maintain it," John said. He didn't want Cheryl to end up in any problems.

"I hear you, John. Well, for now I would need at least one person to help me get started. My assistant in Miami can't, so let's schedule some interviews next and get it started," Cheryl said as she clapped her hands. She was excited; it was something very different and out of the norm for her. Cheryl stayed in the meeting for another hour or so, and then they wrapped things up. She left the conference room and headed for her suite. Business was over; now it was time to party. As Cheryl was walking to the elevator, a tall, sexy, semi-chocolate guy ran smack into her. They hit each other so hard, her papers went one way and her purse another. The hit startled her for a moment. The gentlemen was on the phone when he hit her, so he told whomever it was he had to call them back.

"Hey, let me call you back. I just ran into someone, and I need to make sure they're not hurt." Morris hung up his cell and began to help Cheryl pick up her things.

"Sweetheart, I'm extremely sorry. I honestly didn't see you coming. Are you okay?" Morris asked Cheryl. She wanted to curse his ass out, but my god, he was too damn fine. Instead she stood up. She was trying to speak, but she looked into his bedroom eyes and was speechless. He was so damn fine! He was tall, dark-skinned, and clean-shaven, wearing a low haircut with waves. He was dressed in a black Armani suit; that nigga looked good.

Damn, he is fine! Oh my god. What am I saying? I'm married. Cheryl, snap out of it! Cheryl thought to herself.

"I'm sorry. Yes, I'm fine!" she said as she reached to grab her things from him.

"Are you sure?" he asked as he handed her some of her things. "I'm extremely sorry. I really didn't see you coming my way. And trust me, you are a sight to see," Morris said to her in a flirtatious voice.

Cheryl began to blush after what he said. She found it really corny, but it was something about him. Cheryl had never, ever thought about any man other than her husband the way she was thinking about Morris. She had to snap out of it; she never imagined stepping out on Chuck, but damn.

"It's okay. I guess we both weren't paying attention. But really, I'm okay. Thank you!" Cheryl said.

Morris extended his hand to formally introduce himself. "Well, my name is Morris. What's your name, gorgeous?" he said with a smile on his face.

"I'm Cheryl, and thanks," Cheryl replied.

"Has anyone ever told you, you have a beautiful smile?" Morris said as he smiled at Cheryl.

Cheryl didn't know how to respond. She wasn't really used to this attention, and normally she didn't spend too much time entertaining men and their pickup lines, but she was enjoying this.

"I get that sometimes. Thank you again. Sorry I ran into you. Next time I should pay attention," Cheryl said, and then she giggled.

Morris didn't mind at all. Part of him was a bit happy he ran into her although he knew he was married and shouldn't even attempt to pursue this...but the dog in him had to do it. He had never cheated on his wife, so he said. But lately all his wife did was nag and accuse him, so he was down to engage or converse with someone who would be peaceful. He felt Cheryl was the one to do so with.

"I told you it was my fault, sweetheart, so you should let me make it up to you. How about we go grab a drink or something?" Morris asked Cheryl.

Cheryl was a bit hesitant to answer. She had gotten out of her meeting pretty early, so part of her wanted to say yes, but she didn't want to seem so easy. She turned his offer down, knowing damn well she didn't want to turn him down. "Actually I'm going to have to say no, I can't. I'm in town with a few friends, and they're expecting me."

For some reason, Morris wasn't going to give up so easily. "Well, I hear you, but how long will you be in town? I really feel I owe you at least one drink."

Cheryl was flattered and didn't want to say no. Then she thought to herself, *Fuck that. This dude is fine, and besides, I'm sure Chuck wasn't thinking 'bout me when he was out doing him. And this is so innocent, anyways.* Cheryl always told her clients that two wrongs didn't make it right, but she wasn't trying to follow her own advice at the moment.

"I will be here for a week. I'm not sure if we will have time to hook up." She wanted to make him sweat a little more for her. She thought he would just give up, but he fooled her.

"Okay, that sounds good! I'm here on business myself, and I'll be here for about another week or two. So here is my card. When you get some time, you can call my cell, and we can meet up," Morris told her and then handed her his business card.

Cheryl took the card and read it just to see what his line of business was. The card read, "Becker, Jones, & Johnson, LLC. Morris Becker, Attorney at Law." Cheryl was impressed; she had heard of this firm back in Miami, but she never knew they had an office in LA. She was impressed and surprised at the same time. He was so close yet so far.

"Wow! You're an attorney at Becker, Jones & Johnson, LLC! I'm shocked I've never run into you before. I live in Miami. As a matter of fact, my office is not too far from your firm."

"Yes, that is shocking that we have never run into each other before," Morris replied. He too was shocked that he had never seen Cheryl before. Then again, he probably had but had never paid attention because he only had eyes for his wife. But not today; today his eyes were set on the beautiful woman in front of him. So he and Cheryl chatted a little bit more, and she finally agreed to call him before she left and maybe have a drink with him. They said their goodbyes and went their separate ways.

On Cheryl's way to the suite, she debated on telling Keyshia and Joy about Morris and how she was feeling him, but she preferred to keep that secret to herself for now. She really didn't want to even hear what they would say. Cheryl finally made it to the suite. When she got there, Joy and Keyshia were in the living room watching TV. Before she could get all the way inside, Keyshia started jumping up and down and yelling.

"It's about time, bitch! We are ready to get this party started!"

Joy and Cheryl looked at Keyshia, and all they could do was laugh. She was dancing around and acting a fool.

"Damn, can I at least get settled first? Sheesh. All your ass wants do is party," Cheryl told Keyshia as she walked to sit her things down. Cheryl was ready to enjoy herself, but she wanted to get settled first because that meeting was a bit much for her. She wanted to at least shower and change, and then they could get on with their plans.

"Okay, okay. I hear you," Keyshia said. Then she sat back on the couch.

"So how was the meeting?" Joy asked Cheryl.

"It was cool. We got a lot squared away. By the time I get back home, things should be up and running," Cheryl replied with a satisfied smile on her face.

"That's good. I'm glad to hear that," Joy said.

Cheryl was still smiling and in a daze. She was thinking about Morris and if she should tell her friends about him. But she was like, *Naw, this is one secret I will keep in the dark.*

"I see you are really happy about it; you're just over there smiling," Joy said to Cheryl. If she only knew Cheryl was daydreaming about Morris's sexy ass... Cheryl snapped herself out of it and pretended Joy was right.

"Yes, I really am. All my dreams are coming true although people found what I was trying to do weird. But enough of the business talk! Let's get this vacation started. Let me just take a shower and change, and then we can hit the town," Cheryl said.

Cheryl and the girls finally left their suite. The first stop they made was to grab something to eat. After eating, they decided to go site-seeing—nothing major.

"Wow, this is so damn nice. It feels good to be in a totally different place with no worries or anything," Joy said as she admired everything around her.

"Yes, you can say that again. This shit feels good," Cheryl replied.

Keyshia was too busy scoping out her surroundings. All day she kept talking about how she wanted to meet somebody different and how they should do something wild.

"Look, y'all hos are sounding too boring and shit. Let's really have some fun. Look, y'all both need to get your heads clear. So let's do what we did that time we went to St. Pete," Keyshia said and started to giggle in a mischievous tone.

Joy and Cheryl just looked at her and laughed; they knew exactly what she was talking about. "Bitch, are you serious? We can't be playing like that out here. We are a long way from home," Joy said to Keyshia.

"And that right there validates my point even more."

"Ho, you are really something else. Why does it always have to be something dealing with a nigga? Damn!" Joy said.

Cheryl was just looking at the both of them and laughing.

"Bitch, what are you sitting here laughing for? You're not going to say anything?" Joy snapped at Cheryl, wanting her to back her up.

"Look, maybe Keyshia is right. I mean for you two at least. 'cause I'm still married, so I can't," Cheryl said and burst into laughter. She knew that was going to piss Joy off, but it was all fun and laughs.

See, they went on a trip to St. Pete one year when they were all single and decided to play this damn game called "Random Fuck." They would pick a random dude and have a one-night stand. It may seem like they were hos to most people, but they saw it as all fun and games. Besides, they were in a place where no one knew them, so they really didn't have to worry about seeing the person again. Cheryl was surprised that she had done it back then, and now she was open to the idea. But she didn't want them to know because her "random fuck" would be that damn sexy-ass Morris.

Damn, damn, she thought to herself, but those thoughts were quickly interrupted by Joy slapping her on her arm.

"What the hell, Cher? You can't be fucking serious. And what do you mean for just me and Keyshia? Ho, you are a part of this pack. So if one does it, we all do!" Joy said.

"Well, neither you nor Keyshia is married or attached to anyone, and besides, ho, you need some dick. You've been a bit too fucking moody," Cheryl replied to Joy.

"Now that's the spirit, Cheryl. Tell that bitch again. I mean, we are a pack, but you are married, so you can't fuck. But you can at least talk to someone," Keyshia added and then looked at Cheryl to see what her response would be. She figured Cheryl would say no or come up with some theory of why that wasn't right, but to her surprise, Cheryl agreed.

"Okay, deal! So we can go out later tonight. I will chat with a random dude of your choice, and then we pick your random fucks."

Joy was shocked; she didn't know what had gotten into Cheryl. She felt Cheryl on her forehead, trying to be funny.

"Are you okay? What have you done with my friend?" Joy asked her.

"I'm good, but it's true. I have become a bit uptight, so I just want to get back to the old me. Just a little. So enough talking about this. Let's finish enjoying our day and get ready for tonight."

Chapter Seven

AFTER THEIR DAY OF SIGHT-SEEING, they grabbed some dinner and then went to downtown LA to hit up a club. When they pulled into this club called The Spot, the line was damn near in the parking lot. Now this was the type of shit they saw back home anytime they hit up South Beach. Keyshia was ready as usual. Cheryl really didn't like crowds, but she was ready to let her hair down tonight. By the time they found parking, the line had kind of eased up. Once they got close, they noticed there were two lines. So of course they hit the VIP line. When they got inside to their booth, they glanced around the room. That shit was packed.

"Damn, now this is my type of crowd," Keyshia said as she started bouncing. She was ready to hit the floor.

"Any crowd is your crowd, Keyshia. As long as it includes men, drinks, and music, it's your crowd," Joy told Keyshia.

"Ho, don't judge me," Keyshia replied. Before Joy could offer a rebuttal, a young lady came over. She told the ladies that she would be their VIP server for the night. She opened the bottle of peach Ciroc they had and poured their cups. The ladies sat back and chilled for a bit to let the liquor sit in and to scope out the scene. Once they were feeling right, they decided to leave their section and go to the floor. They got a couple of stares and funny looks from bitches and niggas. You could tell they weren't from there, but they didn't let that shit stop their vibe. The DJ was doing his thing because the music was popping. They danced and juked for a few songs. Then they went to the ladies' room.

"Damn, I'm tired. I haven't danced like that in so damn long," Cheryl said once they got to the ladies' room.

"Girl, me either!" Joy added.

"Wow, this is the nicest club bathroom I've been in," Keyshia blurted out.

"You ain't ever lied. This shit is nice as fuck," Joy said. The restroom was huge, clean, and pretty. It smelled like lavender, and it had some loveseats in a li'l area so you could take a breath.

"Yes, this is nice," Cheryl said as she sat down on one of the loveseats. After they finished freshening up in the restroom, they headed back to their booth to grab some more drinks. They sat there for a few moments, and some dude walked over and asked could he join them. They all looked at each other and smiled. The dude was handsome as fuck, but they had to play hard to get at first. They knew he would try again because they were fresh meat he had never seen in this club before.

"Not right now, sweetie. Maybe later," Keyshia said in a flirty voice.

The dude looked at her, licked his lips, and stared her up and down. "Damn, Ma, as sexy as you are, I will wait. Yes, I sure will wait," he said as he continued to look at her and smile.

Keyshia was looking right as usual. She sported a tight full-body jumpsuit. It was black with the sides cut out to expose her smooth caramel skin. It really complimented all her curves. She wore it well with some red pumps and her hair long down to her butt. She was well accessorized. The dude was damn near drooling as he watched her. Keyshia enjoyed watching him sweat because she kept moving her body and glancing at him. He finally said he'd be back. He felt his manhood jump as he looked at her. He walked off, and they got back to sipping on their drinks. They stayed in the VIP area and just vibed to the music.

Niggas kept coming over trying to holler, and they couldn't blame them; they were looking too good. Joy had on a white sleeveless fitted dress with black stripes and red wedge heels. She, too, had on some nice accessories to bring out the red in her shoes. Cheryl also had on a tight catch-me, fuck-me dress. It was all black, and the back was cut right above her ass. Cheryl was super thick; they always teased her and said her ass was so big like the sun, and she had no waist. They finally went back on the dancefloor. They were really having a blast. Keyshia ended up bumping into the dude who had tried to holler earlier, so she danced all up on him, and they exchanged numbers. After a few more drinks, they decided to leave. They left the club around three in the morning.

That next day, they were scheduled for the Spa at nine o'clock, but they didn't get up until about two that afternoon.

"Damn, I can't believe we slept that long. My head is killing me," Joy said as she headed to the kitchen to grab something to drink. Cheryl and Keyshia had gotten up a little bit before Joy and were sitting at the dining table drinking some coffee.

Keyshia was in a daze, but it really didn't faze her because she was forever going out.

"Y'all really can't hang like we used to, huh? I guess y'all really are getting old," Keyshia stated and started laughing. Cheryl and Joy just looked at her and shook their heads. They sat there for a few more minutes and talked about the night before. Then they decided to head out again that night. This time they went to a male strip club. It was something different to do, and they had a blast. The men were so damn sexy and built. They stayed in the club for a li'l while. After a few drinks and a couple of lap dances, they left. They ended up going to get something to eat at this twenty-four-hour restaurant. Apparently this was the spot everyone went to after they left the club because it was packed.

"Well, dang. This parking lot almost looks like the club parking lot. Sheesh, it's on swoll," Keyshia said.

"It sure is. I hope there is a table for us 'cause I'm hungry as hell, and I don't feel like driving trying to find anywhere else to go," Cheryl told them. It was getting late, and they were tipsy.

"I hear you, and besides, it's not like we're back home. We can't be just driving around; we already don't know where we at," Joy said and chuckled as she checked her face in the mirror. They finally found a parking spot. Before they got out of the car Keyshia thought to herself, *Yes, this is the perfect spot to play our game. Hey, you only live once.*

Joy was about to get out of the car, but Keyshia stopped her. "Hold up, y'all. Okay, I think tonight would be the perfect night for our li'l game," Keyshia said with a smirk on her face.

"Girl, here you go with this bullshit again. Ain't nobody got time for that shit!" Joy said to Keyshia.

Cheryl didn't say a word. She just laughed because she knew what was coming next.

"Damn, Joy, you always want to suck the fun out of things. Shit, we only live once, so why we can't do something spontaneous once in a while?"

"Keyshia, we are doing something spontaneous. We are in a totally different state. Don't get me wrong; I'm in the need of some, but we are older now, and shit is different," Joy tried to tell Keyshia, but she wasn't getting it.

"Different how? It's all fun at the end of the day, something to look back and laugh about." Keyshia was really trying to convince Joy that nothing would be wrong with fucking a random dude. Besides, they had done it before, and it was fun. They would pick the ugliest person for each other to do it with. Joy never saw it funny because she always got stuck with a fat dude.

"Keyshia, don't get me wrong. I hear you, and yeah, we have done it before, but I have a child, and we are getting older. Nowadays, you don't know what these motherfucking niggas got. You need to grow up and stop the shit you're doing. All this having sex with these different men… That shit ain't cool. I…"

Before Joy could finish, Keyshia snapped. She hated when they tried to tell her how she should live her life. "What the fuck do you mean what I need to stop doing? Ho, don't act like you're a saint 'cause not too long before marriage, you were out here fucking and sucking off the chain. So don't even go there with judging me. I'm just saying live a little. No one is pressuring you or forcing you to do anything. I tell you what, let's just drop this whole thing. You do you, and I'mma do me. Let's just enjoy this vacation." Keyshia was heated. She got out of the car and started walking to the door.

Joy and Cheryl sat there for a moment not saying a word. They finally got out of the car, and they all headed inside. After waiting about twenty minutes for a table, they were finally seated. Cheryl noticed a familiar face across the room; it was Morris. She tried to make herself unnoticeable because she didn't want him to see her. She tried to engage in a conversation with her girls, so she wouldn't keep looking his way. "So what are y'all 'bout to order?" she asked as she picked up the menu to take a look for herself.

"Umm, I really don't know what I want. I'm kinda feeling pancakes right now," Joy said as she glanced at the menu. Keyshia didn't say anything. It was obvious she was still upset, so they didn't bother her. The waiter came over, and they ordered their food. After they ate, the girls sat there and chatted for a little while. Keyshia finally got out of her attitude mode. As soon as they got up to leave, Morris and the gentlemen he was with got up and headed for the door. Cheryl saw him headed to the door, and she decided to go to the restroom. She really didn't want Keyshia and Joy to know about him. Although she had not called him yet, this was one secret she was going to keep in the dark. "Y'all, wait a minute. I gotta go to the bathroom," Cheryl told Joy and Keyshia. They followed her to the ladies' room. Morris didn't notice her, so he kept it moving out the door. Cheryl and the girls finally headed back to their suite to get some sleep and prepare for the next day.

The next morning, Cheryl got up and woke Joy and Keyshia. She didn't want them to miss the spa again this morning. "Damn, chick, why are you up so early and waking us up? Shit, it feels like we just went to bed," Keyshia complained as she headed to the kitchen.

"Because I have something planned for us this morning, so stop complaining and just get ready, chick," Cheryl replied. Then she headed to her room to get dressed. She looked back as she headed to the room and smiled at them. Keyshia rolled her eyes and headed to get dressed. About two hours later, the girls were finally dressed and ready to go.

"So where are we going today, chick?" Joy asked Cheryl as she checked her face in her make-up mirror.

"We are going to enjoy a day of pampering. So I'm taking y'all to the spa to get the works. Massage, facial, mani, pedi, everything," Cheryl replied to Joy.

"Damn, girl you must really love us. Now this what you call a fucking vacation," Keyshia said as she did a happy dance.

"I know, right? I'm scared of this new Cheryl," Joy sad and then let out a chuckle.

Cheryl gave both of them a look and said, "I mean, y'all don't have to accept any of this from 'the new Cheryl,' as you said. We can go back home." Cheryl laughed at the look on their faces because they thought she was serious by the tone in her voice.

"That shit not funny. For a minute I thought you were serious, heifer," Joy said and then nudged Cheryl. They all started laughing, and then they headed out the door. Just as they hit the elevators, Cheryl's phone began to ring. She thought it was Chuck and the kids because she had just gotten off the phone with them, but when she looked at her phone, she saw it was an unfamiliar number. She thought to herself for a second, *I sure hope this ain't a damn client. They know I'm on vacation.*

She decided not to answer because she was afraid it was a client, so she pressed ignore. "Who was that? I hope it ain't a client 'cause we're on vacation, trick," Joy said.

"I know we're on vacation. Why do you think I ignored the call? Sheesh. Stop being so damn nosy, chick," Cheryl replied to Joy in a playful tone.

"Well I don't give a damn who call you as long as we're still going to the spa and all that good stuff," Keyshia added as she let out a laugh. She wasn't a bit concerned about all that other stuff. She just wanted to enjoy her time there. Cheryl didn't even respond; she just shook her head and smiled. Joy did the same. They knew Keyshia was all party and play. So the ladies got on the elevator and headed on their way. When they arrived at the spa, their mouths dropped because it was so fucking nice. Cheryl had called ahead and arranged for the spa to be closed to just them for five hours. Yes, they were going to get the works. They each had personalized baskets with their names on them waiting in their own individual section. The baskets were full of goodies for each lady, and they even included a robe with their initials stitched on the front.

"Wow, wow, wow!" That's all Joy and Keyshia kept saying. They had huge smiles on their faces. Cheryl loved the idea of doing things for the ones she loved, and seeing them happy made her feel even better. And by the looks on Joy's and Keyshia's faces, they were beyond happy.

"Cheryl, all this for us? Oh my gosh! Friend, you really did this. Wow! Thank you so much!" Keyshia thanked Cheryl and gave her a hug.

"Y'all are 'bout to make me cry. I'm glad I can make you guys smile, so let's enjoy ourselves, ladies," Cheryl told the girls as she wrapped her arms around them both.

Each of them went to their area and took off their clothes to get ready for their massage. They were scheduled for a one-and-a-half-hour massage each. After the massage, the ladies headed to the room for their facials. After the facial, it was time for lunch. There was a room set up for them with their food being prepared by a private chef Cheryl had hired for them. The ladies took a seat, and a young, muscular, shirtless, dark-chocolate guy wearing pants and an apron came over to pour them some wine.

"Damn. Sexy chocolate, can I have a sip of you in my glass?" Joy said in a flirtatious voice. She couldn't take her eyes off this chocolate sensation standing before her.

"Shit, fuck a sip! Let me get a full glass of you. Damn, you are fine as fuck. Can I touch your sexy body?" Keyshia had no shame in her game, and she was dead-ass serious. The body that stood before her was all that and more, and she just wanted to just feel his skin.

He smiled at her, showing his pearly—and I mean pearly—white teeth and said, "Sure, sweetie. I do not see anything wrong with that." He clearly was loving the attention and the interest they were showing him, so he walked closer to Keyshia, so she could get her feel. Keyshia couldn't help herself; she was rubbing and caressing his chest.

"Damn, you feel so good... Umm, umm, good," Keyshia said as she felt him up even more. Everyone was at the table smiling and giggling. Joy decided to indulge in some of the fun and get her feel on, too. She rubbed her fingers all down his chest.

"Damn, you do feel good," Joy said as she smiled at the server.

Cheryl just sat back and smiled as she watched her girls enjoy the moment. She didn't partake in the fun of feeling the waiter up. This was all for them. Her mind was on someone else; for some reason, watching them with the waiter made her fantasize about Morris. She could picture her body all over his body. Damn, she felt herself get moist again. It was bad enough that she was wet from her massage. For some reason, every time Cheryl got a massage her pussy got dripping wet. Now that she was thinking about Morris, it got even wetter. She had to snap herself out of it. What was she thinking? She was married!

"Alright, y'all, enough foreplay. Let's let him do his job, and let's eat. I'm starving, and we still have a few more hours," Cheryl told Keyshia and Joy.

They really didn't want him to go, but they knew he had to. As he walked away, he turned back and smiled at them. They both nearly melted in their seats.

"Damn, dude was fine as hell. Cheryl, where did you find him?" Keyshia asked Cheryl.

"Don't worry about my connections. I told y'all that I've got y'all. But a collogue of mine referred him, and when I saw the picture of him, I was like, 'Hell yeah, they're going to love him," Cheryl said and then began to chuckle.

"Yes, boo, you really outdid yourself. Shit, my husband hasn't ever treated me to shit like this," Joy added.

Cheryl and Keyshia both looked at her strangely. "What the hell? Why would your husband pick you out a fine-ass dude like that? What type of shit were y'all into? Damn, ho, I knew you was a freak," Keyshia said to Joy.

"Bitch, don't play with me. I ain't talking about that," Joy replied.

"Oh shit. Well, you should have made that clear 'cause we were talking 'bout Mr. Sexy, and you burst out with that," Keyshia said as she began to laugh. All Joy could do was shake her head.

"Girl, I thought the same thing. I'm like, 'Wait a minute! This bitch is tripping,'" Cheryl added.

Joy just kept laughing. "I ain't even going to entertain that nonsense y'all are talking. I can't believe y'all really thought that's what I meant," Joy said and then sipped her glass of wine. The ladies joked around and talked a bit more. After finishing lunch, they headed to get their mani and pedi. The pedicure bath was covered in rose petals, and there were two technicians for each one of them.

"Oooh, this feels so good!" Joy took a deep breath as she closed her eyes to enjoy the pedicure. Cheryl and Keyshia both had their eyes closed as well and were enjoying the feeling and the aroma of lemon-scented candles that flowed through the room.

"Now this is the life. We need to do this more often. My body feels amazing," Keyshia expressed as she kept her eyes closed.

"Yeah, we should. Maybe we can plan something every other month, and we can take turns picking up the tab," Joy added.

"Yeah, but just know when it's my turn, it won't be as extravagant as this shit here. cause I ain't balling like y'all," Keyshia said and then started laughing.

"Trust me, I know your ass wouldn't treat us like this," Cheryl told Keyshia. It wasn't that Keyshia was cheap or anything, but when it came to others, she would not do anything extra that she wouldn't do for herself. But they still loved her and knew she wouldn't mind spending on her friends.

"At least y'all already know," Keyshia teased. "But on the real, we should do stuff like this more often. I know it wouldn't be all the time but at least when we all get free," Keyshia said in a serious and sincere tone. She was always the playful, goofy one, but this time she was serious. So they agreed to talk more about that and set up some plans to do so.

"In the meantime, let's enjoy this moment," Cheryl told them. The ladies sat back, relaxed, and enjoyed their moment. When they were finally done, the ladies felt great. They decided to head back to the suite to chill for a li'l bit till they decided what to do for the night. When they went to grab their things, they all checked their phones.

Cheryl looked shocked that the number that had called her earlier had called her another four times and left messages. She decided to listen to the message. At first she didn't recognize the voice, but the message and the tone made her smile. "Hey, gorgeous. You may not know who this is, but this is Morris. I couldn't get your pretty smile out of my head. So since you haven't called me yet, I took it upon myself to call you. When you're free, hit me up. I really want to take you out for a drink. You have the number, gorgeous. Call me."

Cheryl could do nothing but smile. She was surprised that he had called, and she was also wondering how the hell he had gotten her number. She didn't care how he got it; he had made her day. The sound of his deep, sexy voice replayed over and over in her head.

Damn, what is wrong with me? I'm tripping. I can't be doing this and thinking like this, she thought to herself.

Joy noticed Cheryl smiling and wanted to know what had her cheesing the way she was. "Well damn, bitch. Chuck really must have made your day. I guess he's finally getting back on your good side 'cause, girl, you are glowing," Joy teased Cheryl and started giggling. Cheryl smiled at her, but if only Joy knew that was not Chuck's voice she was listening to... She wasn't going to tell Joy any different, so she went along with it.

"Girl, you know these niggas come to their senses after a while. He's been being real sweet, leaving me messages in his sexy voice and shit," Cheryl replied with a smile. She didn't like lying to her girls, but she knew they would never find out. She was good at keeping secrets, and any secret she wanted to keep safe, she kept it in the dark. There weren't many, but she had a few of them.

"Girl, I feel you. I wish Paul could have done the same," Joy said in a sarcastic tone.

Cheryl knew where that conversation was headed and felt it was best to change the subject because she knew Joy wasn't over Paul and what he had done. It was fucked up and sad how these niggas could be, but she wanted her girl to enjoy the trip. "I hear you, girl, but it's his loss. But let's not get into that. Let's finish enjoying our stay," Cheryl said.

"Yeah, you're right. So what are we getting into next?" Joy asked. Her tone of voice had changed quickly. Cheryl really didn't have much else planned for the rest of the evening, and there was a part of her that wanted to meet up with Morris. She just had to find a way to get rid of her girls. Damn, she hated to be sneaky. This wasn't her at all, but for some reason, she wanted to indulge in this Morris thing some more.

"Yeah, what are we getting into tonight?" Keyshia said. She was ready to party, as usual. Cheryl thought to herself for a moment, and then it hit her. Everyone would be happy. "How about you and Joy go out tonight? I'm going to stay in and talk with Chuck for a bit. I know what you are going to say, Joy, and don't start." Cheryl knew Joy would talk shit because they all were supposed to be enjoying this vacation. But shit, Cheryl was going to enjoy it, too—just not with them for tonight. To her surprise, Joy was cool with it.

"I'm not going to trip. You know I want to see you and Chuck stay together. It gives me hope that one day I will have this special love again. I understand what you are going through, so it's cool," Joy said. Both Keyshia and Cheryl were shocked.

"What? Are you serious? You're not having a bitch fit," Keyshia said to Joy. She knew normally Joy would talk shit about Cheryl bailing out on them, especially while they were on vacation, but she was cool with it and they were shocked. Part of Cheryl felt bad that she was lying to her friends to go meet someone she didn't even know, but she felt it was innocent, so what the hell? Besides, she felt she would let her girls enjoy a night out on the town alone. In case they met someone, she didn't want to seem like she was the third wheel or a cockblocker.

"I'm glad to see you understand, Joy. Besides, y'all need to go have a blast. Y'all might meet someone or something, and I don't want to be that chick who's blocking anything 'cause I'm not the single one. You feel me?" Cheryl said.

"I sure do, boo! Now that's what I'm talking 'bout," Keyshia added. She was down with that because she surely did come to hook up with someone, and she didn't have time to be feeling guilty for leaving her girl hanging.

"Yes, Kesh, we knew that would be fine with you. But I'm cool. Besides, Cheryl, all this is on you anyways," Joy said sarcastically and then started laughing.

Cheryl couldn't do anything but laugh at what Joy said because it was true. Everything was on her. "You know what? Y'all hos just have a good time tonight, and come back in one piece," Cheryl told them.

They stayed in the suite a few hours, and then Joy and Kesh finally left around ten thirty. It was a bit early to them; when they were back home in Miami, they didn't hit the club until about midnight. But because they didn't know their way around,

Keyshia and Joy decided to head out a bit early. As they were leaving, Cheryl was on the couch all into her phone. She was texting Morris, and she had a huge grin on her face.

"Damn, he must have sent you a picture of his dick from the way you're over there grinning! I wouldn't be surprised if he were on a flight on his way up here," Joy teased Cheryl. Cheryl looked at her and started giggling. She knew Joy thought she was smiling because of what she said about Chuck, but she was giggling because Joy had no clue.

"Girl, no he hasn't sent any picture of that, and besides, I don't think his phone has enough space to hold a picture of that," Cheryl said jokingly to Joy.

"Eww, bitch! TMI. Child, please, it better be that big," Joy replied.

Keyshia just looked at the both of them and shook her head. "Y'all bitches need to cut it out," Keyshia said.

"Whatever, hater!" Joy told Keyshia. They teased each other for a li'l bit more, and then Joy and Keyshia finally left. Cheryl was glad. *Damn, it's about time,* she mumbled to herself. Cheryl was supposed to be meeting Morris at some bar for a drink. She hoped she didn't run into Joy and Keyshia since she had let them take the rental and had called a taxi. When she finally arrived to the location, it wasn't really crowded or anything like she imagined it would be, and that made her less nervous about running into to Kesh and Joy. She knew if there wasn't a crowd, Keyshia and Joy would not be there at all. As soon as she got out of the taxi, Morris was standing waiting for her.

He walked over to the taxi to help her out, grabbing her hand. Then he took a step back and looked at Cheryl and said, "Well damn!" He licked his lips and just stared at her. The thoughts that were running though his head…

Cheryl looked damn good as usual. She had on a fitted red dress that was cut low in the front, so it exposed her nice, plump, juicy breasts. Her six-inch red bottoms made her as tall as Morris, and that really turned him on. Cheryl knew what she was doing when she put on that dress; she just wanted to tease Morris. It sure was working because he was damn near drooling. He was speechless. Cheryl loved that she still had that appeal to make a nigga sweat.

"Damn, boo, you look like you just stepped out of a magazine, and you smell so damn good," Morris told Cheryl as he continued to admire her frame.

"Thank you. You look damn good yourself," Cheryl replied to Morris with a flirtatious look on her face. Morris looked and smelled good enough to eat. He had on a dark blue Polo shirt with some sexy denim jeans.

"Is that Armani Mania you wear?" Cheryl asked Morris. She had a thing for men's cologne. She loved a man who smelled good, and she knew her cologne well. Morris was a bit surprised that she picked up on what he had on. Most women would have just complimented that he smelled good.

"I'm impressed you know cologne. Most women just say I smell good and usually ask what I'm wearing. I guess I smell so good they want to get their niggas the same thing," Morris replied and laughed.

"Well, yes. I just love a man who smells good," Cheryl added. They stared at each other for a few seconds. The connection between them was strong. Cheryl snapped out of her fantasy first because the thoughts she was having were so not appropriate. She had to control herself. She knew she wasn't even supposed to be dealing or even out with Morris. So her imaginations of fucking him should be just that—her imagination.

"So shall we head inside?" Cheryl asked so she could break the awkward silence. Morris was still staring at her. Then he motioned for her to step inside. From the outside, you would think this place was some type of shady bar or club, but it was nice and elegant on the inside. It was a nice lounge. It had nice and comfy loveseats in each area, the bar was in the middle of the floor, and the music was good. They took a seat. Morris asked Cheryl, "So what can I get you to drink, cutie?"

Cheryl blushed a little. She didn't want to get anything too strong, but at the same time, she wanted to tease him. "Do they serve sex on the beach?" Cheryl asked Morris in a soft and flirtatious tone. She could tell by the look on his face that he was thinking all types of things.

Morris didn't know how to respond without being offensive. *Damn, she sounds so damn sexy asking for sex on the beach. I sure would give it to her on the beach, or wherever,* Morris thought to himself. Then he smiled at Cheryl with his pearly whites and said, "Sure, sexy, they serve sex on the beach."

"Okay, great. I will have one of those," Cheryl replied.

Morris ordered their drinks, and they began to chat.

"So how long have you been here in LA?" Cheryl asked Morris.

"For about two weeks now. My firm is handling a murder trial, and boy, it's a tough one. I'm defending a guy who was accused of drowning his wife and daughter in their pool," Morris said, taking a gulp of the 1800 he had ordered. Cheryl did not like that stuff; she had had some experiences after taking shots of that.

"Damn, I don't see how you can drink that gasoline. The time I did drink it, that shit had me fucked up for days," Cheryl said. She turned up her nose as Morris took another drink of it. He laughed at her facial expression. Cheryl giggled, and then they continued their conversation. "But wow, that does seem like a pretty tough case. If you don't mind my asking, how long has the trial been going on?" she asked.

Morris decided to joke with her because he wanted to see her smile. He really liked her smile; it was gorgeous. There was something about it that made her so special.

"Well I do mind. That is against my client's confidentiality," he said with a smirk on his face. He got just what he hoped for: Cheryl smiled at him. She figured he was bullshitting because she wasn't asking for detailed information about the case. "Naw, I'm just joking. I just wanted to see your pretty smile," he told her. That made her blush even more.

"Oh, really? Is that so?" she said.

"Yes, that is very so," he said to her with a seductive look on his face. "But to answer your question, it's been about nine months."

"Damn. I know it can be annoying, having to travel back and forth and going over the same thing over and over. How much longer do you suspect it will be?" she asked and then took a sip of her drink.

"Yes it is, but I've been on longer trials, and to be honest, with this one I really don't know. I feel they're just dragging it out 'cause there is not enough hard evidence to really pin him to this. There is another suspect, which is the side nigga. But I have a partner working on it with me, so when there's not a major need for me, he goes to court. So it's not that bad," Morris told her.

"Okay. That seems cool. I've always thought about becoming a lawyer. I even started school for it, but something kept telling me psychology would be a better fit for me. I'm happy with my choice," she said to him.

"But don't you get scared when you dealing with these psycho people?" Morris laughed when he asked her that.

Cheryl couldn't help but laugh at him. "No. I don't work with mental people. I work with family, children, and marriage counseling. Although some of my clients are on the nutty side… "Cheryl joked with him.

"Oh, okay. That's good. So you're the one who has people leave their spouse and shit," Morris teased with her. "My wife tried to get me to go to therapy, but I feel it's a waste of money. No offense to your craft."

Cheryl's suspicion of his being married was confirmed. She could tell by how he spoke that he had done this before. Now she was a bit turned off, but who was she to judge him? She was married, too. This was her very first time going out with someone other than Chuck, so this could've been his first, too. But it was obvious that he and his wife had trouble at home, and Cheryl wanted to be nosy. Besides, maybe she bumped into him to help him. Things happen for a reason, as she always said.

"Why do you feel therapy is a waste?" she asked.

"Because you're paying someone to tell you what to do when you can probably figure it out on your own. And sometimes, there is really no problem, so what's the purpose?" he said.

"I figured you would say something like that, but we don't tell people what to do. We just suggest things, and sometimes it's best to get an unknown third party to help you get a better understanding or a solution. Some people just want someone to listen to them who won't judge them," she told him. Morris nodded his head and said he understood, so they chatted for about another hour. Cheryl looked at the time and noticed it was getting late. She didn't want Joy and Keyshia to beat her to the hotel, so she called Joy and asked where they were.

"We are on our way, 'bout to stop and grab something to eat," Joy told her.

"Okay, cool. I was just checking on you guys. See you soon," Cheryl said. Then they hung up. "Well, it's getting pretty late. I had a great time, but it's time for me to go. I can't let my girls know I was out with another man," she explained to Morris.

"I feel you, ma. So since your hotel is next to mine, I will drive you back. If you have to wait on a taxi, you're not going to beat them there," he told her. She agreed, and they headed to the car. The ride back was a bit silent at first. They both were thinking to themselves about the night and their significant others. Cheryl started to feel a li'l guilty, but she knew it was innocent. Morris really didn't like how silent it was, and he didn't like how his mind was all over the place. So he decided to break the silence.

"So did you really enjoy yourself tonight, Cheryl?" Cheryl was a bit surprised that he actually said her name. She didn't think much of it though.

"Yes, I had a good time. I really enjoyed your company," she said to Morris.

"That's great. I had a good time, too. Part of me wishes the night didn't have to end," Morris told her, and then he paused.

Cheryl didn't know what to say because she felt the same way, but she knew it wasn't right. Besides the fact of her being married, she talked to couples for a living, and it really wouldn't be fair to his wife. But shit, she wished her mind would understand that because the thoughts that were running in her head were the total opposite of what she knew was right. But damn, he was fine, sexy, charming, and successful; he was a great listener, and he could hold a good conversation. He was all the things Chuck used to be and what most women really wanted in a man. Cheryl knew it was only because he was not hers. Who was he, really, to his wife? It was crazy to know that everything she told couples about and suggested they not do was what she was thinking about doing. She decided to go with the flow; she knew how to control herself. At least she hoped she could control herself. Morris noticed she never responded to what he said, so he interrupted her thoughts.

"Are you okay, cutie? You're a bit quiet. Is it something I said?" Morris asked her.

"No, I'm okay! You didn't do anything wrong," she replied.

"Well, what's wrong?" Morris asked again.

Cheryl decided to get to the point. "It's just that this is really awkward for me. We are both married, and I've never stepped out on my husband before, so I just don't want things to go beyond what they should," Cheryl told him. Her tone was soft and sweet, which made it hard for him to listen to the message she was relaying, but he understood her.

"Believe it or not, this is my first time as well, and I never, ever imagined stepping out on her. It's just that lately she's been so damn insecure," he said. He paused for a second and then continued. "It's like every time I turn around, she accusing me of cheating, or she's downing herself by pointing out flaws she has that I've never even noticed. So when I bumped into you, it was just a breath of fresh air. You feel me?" Morris told her.

By the sound in his voice, Cheryl could tell he was sincere and that he was telling the truth. Cheryl had done this for years, so she could tell he was for real. Maybe they did run into each other for a bigger reason. She decided to go with the flow. "I feel you. And that can lead a man to want to go and roam and get that breath of fresh air, but sometimes it can lead to more than it should," she told him.

"Yes, this I know. That's why I've never done this, but when I saw you...I don't know what happened. Don't get me wrong, I love my wife. I've never imagined being without her or hurting her, but the shit she's taking me through gets on my nerves at times," Morris told her.

"Hmm, interesting. So let me ask you, what do you think you do or have done to make her feel the way she does?" Cheryl asked him

"Oh no! This is not about to be a therapy session 'cause I ain't paying you for this!" Morris teased her and laughed. Cheryl looked at him and laughed. "But naw, to be real, I guess it's 'cause of my past. I was a wild nigga before I settled down and got married to her. But besides working hard to provide for us, there is nothing I can really see I do to give her a reason to question my loyalty," Morris told Cheryl.

She could understand where he was coming from, but there had to be more. She wasn't going to pressure him about it. If he was lying, that was on him, so she just went with the flow. "It sounds like so many of my clients. It's tough. But if you love her like you say you do, you will keep trying hard to make it work. Because nowadays, people like to take the sucker way out and give up and start something new, but that's the easy way out. And just because it's someone new, people think it's going to be perfect," Cheryl told him.

Morris heard her and knew she was right. He knew he had some skeletons in the dark, but he wasn't going to reveal them. So he teased Cheryl, so he could change the subject. "Okay, Doctor. I think I'm cured now, so how much do I owe you for this session?" he said. Then he looked over at her and laughed.

Cheryl nudged him in the side and started laughing. She knew he really didn't want to keep talking about his wife, so she backed off. "I see you have jokes," she said.

They arrived at the hotel, and Morris pulled up to the side entrance like Cheryl had asked him to earlier. He put the car in park, and they sat there.

"Well, I really enjoyed this night, Morris."

"Me too. So do you think we can see each other again?" Morris asked her boldly. Cheryl wanted badly to say yes, and his voice only made her panties wetter, but she had to be strong.

"I really don't know if that's such a good idea, and besides, I'll be leaving in a few days," Cheryl told him.

Morris wasn't buying that. By the look on her face, he knew she wanted to say yes, but he understood she had to play hard-to-get. However, Morris was confident in what he did; he knew it may not happen now, but he would get her. "You are probably right, but I just meant as friends or whatnot," he said to her and stared into her eyes. He licked his lips, and that just made her pussy throb. She had to hurry up and get out his presence, so she just went along with it.

"Maybe. I will have to see. If not, we do both live in Miami. If it's meant for us to run into each other again, we will, but it's really getting late. Let me head up," she told Morris. He liked the sound of that and was going to make sure they ran into each other again.

"Yes, you are right, cutie, so let me let you go. But can I at least have a hug?" Morris asked her with a smile on his face.

Cheryl did want to feel his body up against hers, so she agreed. "Sure."

Morris got out of the car, walked around to her side of the car, and opened the door for her to get out. Then they hugged, and he held her so tight, she didn't want to let go. His body felt amazing. Morris could feel his manhood rising as he held onto her soft, smooth skin. It felt so damn good. As they begin to let each other go, Morris kissed Cheryl on the lips—and she didn't stop him, either. His lips were so soft and juicy that it sent chills up her body. They kissed for what seemed like forever. Cheryl didn't want to stop, but she had to. Once they finally parted lips, they gazed into each other's eyes. Neither of them said a word for a few seconds. Cheryl looked at the time on her phone.

"I better go. It's really getting late. Again, thanks. I had a nice time," Cheryl told Morris as she began to walk away. She knew that if she stood there longer, something that shouldn't happen would happen.

Morris checked his watch and noticed it was a bit late, and he knew his wife had probably tried calling him a million times by now. "You're right. We should call it a night. I enjoyed myself as well," Morris agreed. Then he leaned over and gave Cheryl a hug. They said goodnight to each other, and Cheryl headed inside and went upstairs to her suite. Once she got in the door, she leaned against it, and a smile came across her face. She was in a daze thinking about the way Morris's lips felt up against hers. "Damn," she mumbled to herself as she bit her lips. Cheryl snapped herself out of the thoughts. She knew it was wrong, and besides, she needed to get out of those clothes before Keyshia and Joy got back. As soon as she got out the room, Cheryl heard Keyshia and Joy entering the suite. *Thank god I didn't stay out with him any longer,* Cheryl said to herself as she finished getting dressed. Cheryl came out of her room to greet the girls and talk about their night. Once she reached the living room, she saw both of them laid out on the sofa. They both looked beyond drunk.

"Damn, y'all bitches look wasted," Cheryl said to them as she walked towards the love seat to sit down.

"Girl, we had a fucking blast. You should have brought your ass with us," Keyshia told Cheryl as she bounced up and down on the couch. Cheryl looked at Keyshia and just started laughing.

"I can tell y'all had a blast 'cause, bitch, you're still crunk!" Cheryl said and laughed. "I'm glad, and don't worry. Tomorrow night, we are going to party hard," Cheryl told Keyshia.

Joy was really out of there; she had passed out on the couch. Cheryl and Keyshia looked at her and burst into laughter. Joy never really could hang, and especially not with Keyshia. That chick was a party animal. "This girl knew she couldn't hang. She is gone! We should get her ass. She's always talking all that shit!" Keyshia said with a devilish look on her face.

Cheryl already knew what Keyshia was talking about. She knew Joy would be pissed the hell off when she got up if they did that. Normally Cheryl would try to stop Keyshia, but she was still high off her night with Morris and that kiss. So she agreed to help Keyshia. They went and got everything you could name: mayo, jelly, ketchup, mustard, oil, and some other shit out the kitchen. They mixed some of it together in a bowl and then started putting it in Joy's hands and all over her body. Then they took a string and started dangling it over her face, making a buzzing sound. Each time they did that, Joy would slap herself in the face smearing what was in her hands all over her face. Cheryl took out her phone and took a picture of Joy. She looked fucked up; her face was covered in shit, and her mouth was wide open. Keyshia and Cheryl stood there looking at her, just laughing. "Now this bitch should know better than to get drunk and pass out around us...well, especially around me," Keyshia said and continued laughing. Keyshia and Cheryl sat and talked a little more about the club. Then they left Joy passed out and fucked up on the couch.

Chapter Eight

THAT NEXT MORNING CHERYL AND Keyshia were awakened by the piercing sound of Joy screaming like somebody was trying to kill her. Cheryl and Keyshia both jumped up and ran out of the room to go see what the hell was going on. Joy was standing in the middle of the kitchen just screaming when they came speeding around the corner to see what was wrong. Joy had dashed a bucket of ice-cold water on them both, taken a cup of stuff she had mixed together with some of everything in it, and poured it on them. Keyshia and Cheryl just stood there soaking wet, staring at Joy like she was crazy.

"Bitch, what the fuck is wrong with you, pouring this shit on me early in the fucking morning? You're standing here…"

Before Keyshia could finish, Joy cut her off. "The same thing that was wrong with y'all silly bitches last night when y'all decided to be stupid and put all that shit on my face and stuff!" Joy yelled at Keyshia and then walked out the kitchen, leaving Keyshia and Cheryl standing there. She headed to the room. Cheryl and Keyshia both just stood there as if they were shocked by Joy's actions. They knew she would be pissed, but she looked and sounded beyond pissed. Cheryl turned and looked at Keyshia with a clueless look on her face, but Keyshia was mad.

It was too early in the morning for her to have to deal with that bullshit. Cheryl, on the other hand, had known Joy would retaliate, but she didn't expect her to be so quick. But it was cool; Cheryl wasn't mad, and she just laughed it off.

"Cher, this shit is not funny. This bitch is tripping early in the morning," Keyshia said to Cheryl.

"Look, we can't be mad at her. Look what we did to her. We just have to suck it up and deal with it. Now I'm about to go get cleaned up because we've got things to do," Cheryl told Keyshia. Then she walked away and headed to the room. Keyshia really didn't want to hear that shit, but it was true. She couldn't get mad at Joy, so she just chuckled to herself and walked to her room.

About two hours later, they were all dressed and ready to head out. As Cheryl was gathering her purse and things, her phone started buzzing. It was a text message. She thought it was Chuck because he had been calling her all morning, but she really wasn't in the mood to talk. She knew the kids were fine, so she didn't see an urgent need to speak with Chuck. Besides, all he kept doing was calling and saying how sorry he was and how he didn't want to lose her and shit like that. Cheryl was sick of hearing that same shit over and over, but she went to grab her phone anyways just to see if it was really Chuck or not. To her surprise it was not Chuck; it was Morris's sexy ass.

The text read, "Good morning, sweet lips. You have been on my mind all night. I know it's not right, but damn, there's just something about you that does something to me. I just wanted to wish you a good day, and I hope I hear from you again."

Cheryl stood there staring and smiling at the text. She read it over and over again. All she could do was replay the kiss in her head and remember how moist it got her. Shit, just thinking about it got her pussy moist. Damn, she knew it was wrong, but it feel so right. *Naw, this shit is crazy. I can't be doing these things. I talk to about this same stuff people for a living. I've gotta snap myself out of it,* she thought to herself as she read and smiled and stared at the phone. She was just about to write him back, but Joy and Keyshia came in the room.

"Damn, Cher, what are you doing? Hurry your ass up," Joy said to her as she walked further into the room. Keyshia noticed the look on Cheryl's face as she was walking in the room.

"No wonder shit's taking forever. She was in here caking with Chuck," Keyshia said playfully. Cheryl smiled; if they only knew that he wasn't even on her mind at the time.

"Well, I know y'all have got an issue, but we're on vacation. Come on, bitch. Let's go. You two will have all the time to make up. Besides, aren't you the one who has said space makes the heart grow fonder?" Joy said to Cheryl in a sarcastic tone and gave her a funny look.

Cheryl didn't utter a word. She just looked at them, laughed, and then grabbed her purse and keys. "Girl, you're a trip. Man, let's go," Cheryl said, and they all walked out of the room and headed out. When they got on the elevator, Cheryl decided to text Morris back. She really didn't know what to say, so she just went with whatever came to mind. "Well, good morning to you to, mister. You were on my mind as well. I really don't know what to say, but I really enjoyed our night. You have a good day as well, handsome." Cheryl pressed send and smiled. The girls really weren't paying her any attention. They were too busy updating their Instagram and Facebook statuses. They finally reached the car, and Cheryl let Keyshia drive while she gave her directions. Their first stop was to get something to eat, and then they had to go tear the mall down.

"Woohoo! Now this is what I'm talking 'bout. This wouldn't have been a vacation if we didn't hit up the mall!" Keyshia said in an excited tone.

When they finally finished shopping, they each had at least nine bags apiece from different stores and had to have someone help them bring the rest. Cheryl was all smiles. She was having fun and enjoying the time spent with her girls.

"All this shopping I did worked up an appetite," Joy said and chuckled. "I was just thinking the same thing. Girl, a bitch is starving!" Keyshia added.

"Well, let's drop these things off and then go get something to eat," Cheryl said. A few hours later after they had finally finished shopping and eating, they went back to their suite and sat back for a while until it was time for them to head out that night. They got ready and headed to some club a friend of Cheryl's had told her about. When they got there, it was packed. The line was halfway in the parking lot, and they could barely find parking. Inside the club was really nice, and the DJ was doing his thing. The ladies scanned the room to see what the crowd was looking like, and it was thick.

"Damn, Cheryl, you sure picked a good spot. This shit is thick as fuck!" Keyshia said to Cheryl as she tried to yell it to her over the music.

"Yes, you sure did," Joy added as she started bouncing to the sounds of the music. They headed to the bar and got a few drinks. Like at every other club, there were a few what they called "thirsty-ass chicks and niggas" in the building, but they didn't pay them any mind. They just partied. Keyshia was damn near wasted, but she had her eye on some guy who was cross the room looking and smiling at her.

"I think I found my random fuck for tonight," she said to Joy and Cheryl as she stared into his direction and smiled.

"Are you serious with this random fuck bullshit, Keyshia? Your ass needs to stop this shit. It's too much…"

Before Joy could finish, Keyshia cut her off. "Listen, bitch, don't start with that judging me bullshit. I'm a grown-ass woman, and I can do what the fuck I want. I don't go around telling you who to fuck or what to do just because you chose to stay single and lonely and weep over that nigga. So let me do me, and you do you," Keyshia said to Joy and walked off. Joy was speechless and pissed at the same time. She was just trying to look out for Keyshia.

"Look, before you say anything, just leave her be. You know how she gets. We can only hope and pray she is safe. Besides, we're here to have fun, so let's do that," Cheryl told Joy. She could tell by the look on Joy's face that she was about to go after Keyshia, and they would end up arguing back and forth. Cheryl really didn't want that to happen, so she tried to nip it in the bud quickly. As the night went on, the ladies enjoyed themselves. After the club, Keyshia sure enough left with the random dude. Cheryl and Joy both tried to stop her, but she wasn't trying to hear that.

"Look, you only live once. I'm single and in a different city, and I know how to protect myself. Yeah, both of y'all and others may call me a ho or whatever, but I'm grown, and trust me, I protect myself. It may look like I fuck every nigga I meet, but I really don't. I'm just doing me," Keyshia said to them. Then she hugged them both and walked off.

There wasn't anything they felt they could do to convince her differently, so they let her go, and they headed to the suite. Once they got there, Joy took a shower and went straight to sleep. Cheryl, on the other hand, couldn't sleep knowing Keyshia was out there, so she got on the phone with Morris. They were on the phone for about three hours straight, just talking, and she was enjoying every moment of it. They learned so much about each other. They finally ended their conversation, so they both could get some sleep. A little while later, Keyshia came creeping in the door. She just went straight to her room and made sure no one heard her. Once she got in her room, she went in the bathroom, closed the door, got in the shower, and cried. She had been raped.

The following morning, the ladies went to get something to eat—except for Keyshia, who stayed in her room. She was too hurt and embarrassed. Keyshia told herself that this was one secret that she would let stay in the dark. For the next few days before they left to head back home, they just chilled and toured the city. Keyshia wasn't her normal self, and Joy and Cheryl noticed that but didn't want to bother her. They finally made it back home to Miami. Joy couldn't wait to get to her daughter. She hated the fact that she would be with her ex and his new bitch. She wasn't the type of chick to keep her child from seeing her father, but she sure did miss her. Keyshia headed home. She still wasn't really saying much because she didn't want to hear the "I told you SOS."

Cheryl, on the other hand, had to meet with a client, but she missed her kids, so she called Chuck and told him to bring the kids and meet her at the park. She had a little time before her appointment, so she decided to spend it with her kids. Once Chuck got there, the kids jumped out of the car and ran straight to her. Cheryl was so excited to see them. She gave them each a big hug. When Chuck finally walked up, she glanced at him and just kept playing with the kids. When it was time for her to go, she didn't want to leave the kids, but she knew she had to make this money. She gave the kids a big hug and kiss and told them she would see them later. Chuck looked at her in hopes that she would hug him, too. Cheryl really didn't have any intentions of hugging him, but she didn't want the kids to know anything was wrong, and part of her missed him a little, so she gave him a hug and a kiss. He smelled so good, and she liked that. Chuck was happy to have her in his arms, and he whispered in her ear, "Baby, I love you, and I'm sorry." Cheryl didn't say anything back. She kissed him again, left, and headed to her car.

Once she reached the office, she sat in her car for a moment to catch her breath and gather her thoughts. She had to get it together because all she was thinking about was Morris at the moment. She knew she had to get it together because she was just about to meet a new client. Plus, she had a few e-mails to answer from her virtual clients, so she really needed to be focused. As she walked in her office, her assistant greeted her in a cheerful tone.

"Well hello there, Missus. I must say I did miss you while you were gone," she said to Cheryl. Cheryl smiled because she felt the same way.

"Hey, sweetie. I missed you, too. I really wish you could have joined me. It was fun," Cheryl said to her assistant and then leaned in to give her a hug.

"Yes, I sure wish I could have, but maybe next time," her assistant stated with a grin on her face. "Here are your messages, and your new client is already in your office waiting for you. I must say, damn! He is fine as fuck. Oops, excuse my language, boss lady," she teased with Cheryl.

"Girl, you're a trip. What is his name again?" Cheryl asked her assistant.

"He told me his name was Beck, and my, my, my… Beck sure is sexy. Please tell me if he is leaving his spouse. I just want to tap that." Cheryl's assistant was clearly feeling whoever the dude was, but Cheryl knew that she was joking, so she really just joked back with her.

"Now, you remember the rules: doctor-patient confidentiality," Cheryl told her. Then they both laughed, and Cheryl headed to her office. When she opened the door, the gentleman was sitting at her desk in her chair with his back facing the door. Cheryl was shocked at how comfortable he looked all laid back in her chair, but damn, he smelled good. Cheryl shook her head and then closed the door loud enough to get his attention, but he didn't budge. So she walked closer to her desk and cleared her throat. When she did that, the chair slowly began to twirl around. Once it was completely facing her, Cheryl's jaws dropped as she saw the figure that was sitting in front of her. She was speechless; she didn't know what to say or do. The person in the chair could tell she was surprised by the expression on her face.

"I take it by the look on that gorgeous face that you are very surprised to see me," Morris said to her in that sexy voice of his. Cheryl was still a bit stunned by seeing him she wondered if he was actually coming for advice or just coming to see her. She didn't know what to do or say, so Morris decided to break the awkward silence in the room. "I know you are wondering what I'm doing here."

"You are sure right about that," Cheryl finally spoke. She really wanted to know to know the reason for this visit.

"Well, to be honest, I couldn't stop thinking about you, and I knew once you got back here, I wouldn't get a chance to see that pretty face and sexy frame, so I called and scheduled a session," Morris said to her and smiled, showing all of his pearly whites. He had a great smile, one you couldn't help but love. So much in Cheryl wanted to be mad at him, but she kind of liked that he had gone through all that to see her. Part of her knew it was wrong, but for some reason she went with the flow.

"Oh, really? So you needed to see me so bad that you had to schedule a fake meeting?" Cheryl asked him.

"Yes, really. That is so right, and I'm very glad I did. You look amazing," Morris said to her in a soft tone and licked his lips. He was looking at Cheryl like she was a plate of dessert, and he was ready to dig in. He walked from around the desk and headed closer to her.

"Thank you, and I must say, you look damn good yourself," Cheryl told him. "So what do you want to talk about, Mister? Oh, and I hope you know I charge by the hour," Cheryl teased him and laughed.

Morris couldn't help but laugh, and he loved her voice. It really turned him on. "Oh, yes, ma'am. I know all about your payment requirements. It's all taken care of, sweetie," Morris said to her in a flirtatious voice. It was obvious that they were flirting with each other. Cheryl was a little nervous, but she was enjoying every moment of it.

Morris came up close to her, grabbed her things out of her hand, and placed them on the chair. Her body tensed up as he got closer. She closed her eyes and inhaled as she felt the warmth of his body up against hers. Then he took his soft lips and began to kiss her softly on her neck. Cheryl could feel the juices in her pussy flowing, and it was throbbing. She wanted to tell him to stop, but the words wouldn't come out. Morris could tell by the way her body was tensed that she was nervous. He was nervous, too, but it was something about her. He just had to have her.

He took his fingertips and trailed them up and down her legs. Cheryl took a deep breath and let out a soft moan. She felt the bulge in his pants move, and oh boy, was it big. He started kissing her on her lips, and she kissed him back. Each time she felt his tongue, she loosened her body up. "Do you want me to stop?" he whispered softly to her in between kisses.

Cheryl replied, "No!" Then she let out another soft moan. By now, her panties were dripping wet. Morris then took his hand and ran it between her legs, and he could feel her wetness dripping through her panties down her thighs. Cheryl moaned louder. Morris was amazed at how wet she was; he had never experienced wetness like this before. Cheryl was like a running faucet, and Morris wanted to be the cup that caught every drop of her juices.

"Damn, ma, you're soaking wet and warm," he whispered to her. Then he moved and directed her body towards the love seat she had in her office. He gently laid her down on it, and then he spread her legs and ran his fingertips up and down them. Cheryl moaned and arched her back. She loosened her body up even more. Morris slid her panties down to her ankles and then all the way off. He then inserted two fingers inside her pussy. "Damn, baby, this pussy is warm and juicy," Morris whispered to her as he stuck his fingers in and out of her juicy, throbbing pussy.

"Oh, really, so you like that?" Cheryl responded in a sexy tone.

Morris started sucking on her breast and kissing her before making his way down. He started kissing her inner thigh. Cheryl moaned more and started rubbing his head. She then whispered to him, "What are we doing? What if we get caught by my assistant or someone?"

That's what's going to make this moment great," he said to her in between kisses. He then started licking the juices between her legs. That was driving Cheryl crazy, and she forgot about everything else. She was on another planet. His lips and tongue felt so good and soft. Morris then started sucking on her clit and tasting all of her. Cheryl was dripping wet, and Morris was enjoying every moment of it. Cheryl's body begin to tremble, and her breathing got faster.

"Oh, Morris, I'm cumming. Damn, this feels so good. Ooh, shit, I'm cumming," Cheryl told him. She shook and wiggled her body as she began to cum all in his mouth. When she came, Morris was sucking and licking up all her juices. Once he finished, he stood up in front of her. Cheryl unzipped his pants, grabbed his dick, and started stroking it with her hands. Then she licked around the head of his dick, teasing him at first.

"Damn, this is a whole lot of meat," she said to him. Morris closed his eyes and smiled. Cheryl began to suck on just the head at first. Then she deep-throated all eight inches of him.

"Damn, ma, that feels so damn good," he said.

Cheryl took his dick in and out of her mouth and started spitting on it to wet it up even more. "Yes, wet this dick, baby." Cheryl started sucking harder and faster. This was driving Morris crazy. He stopped her and told her he wanted to feel her. He turned her around and bent her over. All he could see was her fat, wet, throbbing pussy.

"Damn!" Morris said as he took a step back and looked at her pussy. He positioned himself behind her and eased his way inside of her. First he stuck just the head in. Cheryl was tight and wet. "Damn, girl, this pussy feels good," he told her. Morris kept sticking his dick in and out, teasing her pussy. Each time he did that, Cheryl's pussy throbbed and gripped his dick.

"Ooh, fuck me, Morris. Ooh, yes. Get this pussy, baby. Damn, it feel so good," Cheryl told him in between her panting. Morris was enjoying every moment of it. He had his eyes glued to her, as he was biting down on his bottom lip. Cheryl was throwing it back like a pro.

"Damn, girl, get this dick. This pussy feels so good," Morris said. Then he slapped her ass to give her more motivation, and that's exactly what it did. Her pussy started throbbing even more, and she was throwing it back faster. Her nice, plump ass was clapping and bouncing on that dick. The both of them were breathing fast and moaning.

How could something so wrong feel so perfect? Cheryl thought to herself. She was enjoying the moment but was nervous at the same time. She feared getting caught by her assistant or someone else. "What if what if we get caught?" Cheryl struggled to say in between her moaning and fast breathing.

"That's what's making this feel so right, the fear of getting caught. And, baby, I don't care 'cause this feels so damn good. Damn, this pussy's good. That's right, throw that pussy back, baby."

"Ooh, it feels so good. I'm cumming, Morris. Morris, I'm cumming. Oh my god!" Cheryl blurted out as her body trembled.

"Yes, cum all over this dick, baby," Morris replied back to her as he pounded faster and harder. He was cumming, too. They both reached their climax, and both their bodies went limp. They both lay back on the couch for a few minutes. Then Cheryl got up, went inside her bathroom, and closed the door. She stood in front of the mirror, and tears filled her eyes. She couldn't believe what she had just let happen. She really didn't know how or what to feel at that moment. Cheryl knew it was wrong, and part of her felt guilty. However, she felt so good; it was the best sex she had had in a while. Cheryl stood there and closed her eyes, replaying each moment that had just happened. Her thoughts were interrupted by a knock on the bathroom door.

"Are you okay?" the voice of the guy that just given her the time of her life asked her.

"Yes, I'll be out in a minute," she replied to him. Cheryl washed herself up and left the restroom. When she opened the door, Morris was standing right in front of the door with nothing but his T-shirt on. Damn, he looked so delicious. It made Cheryl think about tasting him again, but she knew that couldn't happen. Morris looked her up and down and licked his lips. He was clearly thinking the same thing by the way he was looking at her. She smiled and then walked past him to go get dressed. Morris watched her from the bathroom door, and then he went inside to clean himself up.

After they got dressed, Cheryl sat at her desk, and Morris sat across from her. They were silent for a while until Cheryl looked at the time. She had another client coming soon. Plus, she needed to respond to some online clients. "Hey, I have another client coming in a few, and I need to get myself prepared."

That's not really what she wanted to say, but she didn't really know how to say anything now. She was still a bit shocked.

Morris could sense her vibe, so he decided to respect her wishes. "Okay, sweetheart. I understand, and besides, I need to get to the office. I have court this evening. I hope to see you again," Morris said to her as he got up out of the seat and walked towards her.

Cheryl didn't know how to respond. Part of her wanted to say "Hell yeah," but she knew that she shouldn't. But damn, he put the dick down right, and he was so damn fine. "I'm not sure. We will see what happens," she said to him in an unsure tone. She didn't want to give him hope, but she also didn't want him to think she didn't enjoy what had just happened. So she kept it simple. He respected what she said and knew where she was coming from. He then grabbed his coat, gave her a hug, and headed out the door.

Cheryl plopped down in her chair and then buried her face in her desk. All she could do was think about what had just happened. It was crazy. Yes, of course it felt good, and it was just what she needed, but it was wrong. They both were still married, and she was supposed to know better. Her thoughts were interrupted by a knock on her office door. She raised her head quickly and glanced in the mirror to make sure she was presentable. Then she told them to come in.

"Hey, boss lady. Your next appointment called and said she will be running a little late, and I checked the website, and you have a few messages," her assistant told her. Cheryl was a bit relieved that her appointment would be late because her mind still wasn't all there. Even while her assistant was talking to her, Cheryl's mind drifted off to the prior activities that took place in her office. *Damn, it was so good, though. It's strange that what feels so good is so damn wrong,* Cheryl thought to herself and then shook her head. Her assistant was steady talking, and Cheryl was trying to pay attention. Then her assistant started talking about Morris, and that caught Cheryl's attention. "So what's the story with Mr. Sexy? When he walked out, he seemed to have been pretty pleased with your services from the way he was smiling when he left your office. So does that mean he is getting a divorce?" her assistant asked her in a joking way. Little did she know, Morris was very pleased but not with the kind of services she was thinking. Cheryl brushed her off quickly.

"Now, you know the rules," Cheryl told her and chuckled.

"Of course. Doctor-client confidentiality or whatever that crap is," she replied in a sarcastic tone. She really wanted to know, but Cheryl wouldn't tell her anything. So she just changed the topic.

After meeting with her next client, Cheryl took a break to go over a few notes. Her phone rang. She assumed it was Chuck, but again to her surprise, it was Morris. She really didn't want to ignore him, but talking to him right now wasn't a good idea, so she sent him to voicemail. Besides, she had a lot of work to do, and she needed to be focused. After ignoring his call, Cheryl decided to just turn her cell completely off. She took a deep breath, closed her eyes to gather her thoughts, and then she got to work.

Chapter Nine

SHE WENT ONLINE TO REVIEW and answer some of the questions a few people had sent her. As she went through a few of the questions, some just made her shake her head at the things people asked her advice about. One woman asked:

What to do? My boyfriend wants to have a foursome, with me, him, my sister, and her boyfriend. I really love him, but I don't know what to do. He said if it doesn't happen, he's going to leave me. I asked my sister, and she was really upset. She thinks I'm trying to find an excuse to have sex with her boyfriend, but that's not true. So what should I do? Should I try to convince my sister to do it? I really don't want to lose him. Help me, please.

Signed, CrazyInLove

Cheryl responded:

Dear CrazyInLove,

First off, you have the right name: Crazy in Love. You are. To be honest, your boyfriend has either been wanting your sister, or he is just a complete jackass. Excuse me, but he clearly doesn't love you the way you love him. Because if he did, there is no way in hell he would ask you that. Now, I know men ask their women for threesomes, but not with your sister. That's just downright disrespectful and nasty.

You need to tell him hell fucking no! There is no way you're going for that. If he loves you, then he will say okay and that he is sorry. If he doesn't care, then he will move the fuck on. I know you love him, but apparently there is no respect on his end. So it is up to you, baby girl. Just always remember, any choice you make in life, you have to live with the outcome. If you allow him to get away with this, you are only opening up more doors for him to try you. Make a choice that you can live with and a choice that is best for you. Hope this helps.

Keep in touch. Love, Cher

Now that was crazy. I hope what I said helped 'cause I really didn't know what to say, Cheryl thought to herself. She decided to answer a few more before she left for the evening.

Dear Cher,

What do I do? I have a boyfriend, and I really love him. He says he isn't cheating on me. For some reason, I get the feeling that he is, but I am not sure. Before we dated, I knew he was sort of a player, but he is so sweet and kind to me. He treats me like a queen, but I don't know. What do I do? Do I trust him, or what?

Signed, Logan Luv

Dear Logan Luv,

A relationship is built on trust, and if you don't trust him, then there is no foundation for your relationship. You have to learn to trust him, honey. Now, I know with men who are charming, it's hard to do and to know what's real. I mean, you don't want to keep assuming and then find out that you are wrong and lose a great guy. If you care for him, you will give him a fair chance to prove to you that he is not cheating on you. Life is full of risks that we have to take whether we want to or not, but that's the only way we can get through life. If he has done something or is doing something to make you feel this way, then let him know instead of accusing him. To be real with you, if you knew he was a player before you two started dating, then you should have known better and known what to expect. You knew you were not going to trust him based on his past the possibility that he will cheat. Believe it or not, some people can change. He may have gotten with you and really realized how important it is to treat a woman well. Maybe he's not cheating on you—who knows? Like I said, it's just a risk you have to take. If you care for him and you are willing to give him a chance, go ahead. But if you have your doubts and in your heart you feel he is cheating, then follow your heart, and do what you feel is right—even if it means you leave him. The choice is up to you. You just have to follow your heart to find your own destiny. Just make sure that your heart matches your mind and your mind matches your mouth.

Keep your head up.

Cher

Dear Cher,

Do you think he cares about me? Cher, I'm in love, but it's so hard. I wish he could tell me how he feels. I don't know what to say. I've got so much to say and so much to give him. I wish he knew how I felt. I want to tell him, but I'm afraid of the outcome.

Melissa in Love

Dear Melissa in Love,

All you have to do is start from the beginning. Have a heart-to-heart talk with him, and let him know how you feel. You have to open up to him. That's the only way you will find out if he cares for you. Just be natural, be yourself, express your feelings, and don't be sacred. A closed mouth can't be heard.

Express your feelings.

Love, Cher

After finishing up with her work, Cher decided to call it a day. She was ready to go home and relax. On her way out the door, Chuck called her. This time she answered. "Yeah," she said when she answered the phone. That pissed Chuck off.

"Damn, that's how you greet your husband? Shit. By the tone of your voice, you sound annoyed. If you didn't want to talk to me, you should have ignored my fucking call like you've been doing all day," Chuck told Cheryl. He was clearly sick of her attitude and the way she was acting towards him. He knew he fucked up, but shit, he said sorry. He was trying to make it up to her. She made the choice to give him another chance, but she was not even giving him a fair chance.

"Shit. How much longer are we going to go through this?"

Cheryl wasn't in the mood to go back and forth with him. Besides, she didn't give a fuck how he felt. He was the one who fucked up. "Look, I ain't in the mood to argue. You called for a reason, so what's up?" Cheryl replied. That pissed Chuck off even more, so he just hung up.

Cheryl heard her phone beep, and she looked down in shock. "I know this stupid motherfucking didn't just hang up on me," she said out loud to herself, still looking at the phone. She waited a few seconds to see if he could call back. She thought maybe the call had dropped. After a few minutes had passed by and he didn't call back, she knew her first thought was right. "That bitch really hung up in my fucking face." She wanted to call back and go off on his ass, but he would probably hang up again. "I've got something for that bitch when I see him."

Cheryl continued to get ready to leave the office. She stopped by her assistant to give her some instructions. "Okay. Well, that's all. I will see you tomorrow. Oh, and remember I'm scheduled to leave for LA in two weeks. Make sure you book the flight and rearrange my appointments. I will only be gone for three days, or maybe two."

"Cool, boss lady. I'll make sure I take care of it. See you tomorrow."

Once Cheryl got in her car, she took a deep breath. She still had the events with Morris on her mind. Yeah, it sure felt good, and part of her saw no wrong in it since Chuck had cheated on her with who he cheated with. But deep down, she knew that two wrongs didn't make a right and stooping to that level didn't prove anything. At the end of the day, she would still be with Chuck, and Morris would be with his wife.

Just as she tried to shake it off, clear her mind and prepare herself for home, her phone rang. She thought it was Chuck calling back, but it was Mr. Morris. "Oh my gosh!" she yelled. Then she took a deep breath and answered.

"Hello," she said in a dry tone. Morris picked up on her attitude.

"Wow, like that? What's wrong, sweetheart? Is it something I did wrong?" he asked.

Cheryl let out a chuckle. "You can't be serious, dude."

"What is that supposed to mean?" he replied.

"Nothing, Morris. This is just really awkward and not right. Don't get me wrong, I like you, and you are one hell of a guy, but we both know this is wrong. And if this were to get out and we got caught, it wouldn't be good for either one of us," she explained to him.

Morris was listening, and he felt where she was coming from, but there was really something special about her. He just liked her. "Baby, I understand. Trust me, I do. But damn, how could something that feels so good and right be wrong? I know it's wrong, but there is a reason we met and this happened. If it wasn't supposed to happen, it wouldn't have," he said to Cheryl. He was trying to convince her that it was fate that brought them to this, but Cheryl wasn't the type to be easily convinced.

"You are really funny. So we met by fate? Really?" Cheryl said to him sarcastically. They both laughed at what she said. Then Cheryl got serious. "No, but for real, I don't know 'bout all that fate stuff, but I know we can't do this. It was a pleasure meeting you, but…"

Before she could finish, he cut her off. "Save the rest for the next time we see each other. I will leave you on this note. I guarantee you we will meet again. And no, I'm not going to come to your office or anything like that. But just watch what I tell you. Remember, it's fate baby." he told Cheryl. She couldn't do anything but laugh at his sense of humor, and that made her wonder.

Is it fate? Now this is crazy, she said to herself. "Okay, Mr. Fate, I have to go. Like I said, it was a pleasure, and you take care," Cheryl said to him.

"Wow, baby girl. You're really speaking like we're not going to speak again, but I will go with the flow, and you will see. So you have a great day, too, and remember your secret's safe with me," Morris said. Then they hung up, and that was the last time they spoke for a while.

Chapter Ten

SINCE THEY HAD BEEN BACK from the trip, Keyshia had not spoken to the girls in about a month or so. She hadn't even been out clubbing. She was not her normal self at all. Joy had been blowing her up all morning, but she just kept ignoring her calls and everyone else's. She had a secret inside, and part of her wanted to tell it, but she figured it was best to keep it in the dark. Keyshia didn't want anyone judging her although she did miss her friends. She knew she couldn't avoid them for too long, so she just decided to talk to them, but she wasn't going to speak of what had been going on with her. There was no way they could find out anyway, so she figured her secret was safe. Keyshia finally called Joy back to see what was up.

"What's up, bitch?" Keyshia greeted Joy once she answered.

"I need to be asking you what's up. Bitch, I haven't heard from you since we got back. I know you ain't mad still 'cause I thought we was cool," Joy said to Keyshia.

"Bitch, no! I've just been really busy lately. That's all. My bad. But what have you been up to? Are you free? I wanted to go have lunch," Keyshia asked Joy. She really didn't want to. She only asked so that she could pretend she wanted to. Deep down she was hoping Joy would say no, but her wish was not granted.

"Yes bitch, cause I'm starving. I have a taste for some seafood or something. Ooh, how 'bout Joe's Crabshack?" Joy replied.

"Okay, cool. Do you want to meet there or at your house?" Keyshia asked.

"We can meet at my house. Have you talked to Cheryl today? I wonder if she wants to join," Joy asked. Now Keyshia already really didn't want to deal with her. What made her think she was really in the mood for both of them?

"No, I haven't, but I doubt she is going to want to ride way up this way for lunch, especially if she is at her office," Keyshia said quickly, chopping that idea.

"You're right. Maybe we can meet up with her later in the week. Well, let me get ready, and I'll see you in a few," Joy said. Then they hung up.

About an hour later, Keyshia finally made it to Joy's house. Joy met her at the door. "Damn, bitch, it took you long enough. I'm starving. Let's bounce."

Keyshia just shook her head, and they headed to the car. The ride there was a bit quiet. They only spoke briefly about the trip and how they had fun. Keyshia really didn't want to speak about it, but she entertained it for the moment. Once they got there, they were seated, and they ordered drinks. Keyshia didn't order any alcohol as she normally did. "I'll take a fruit punch with light ice," she told the waiter.

Joy had a surprised look on her face, and Keyshia really didn't like it. "What the fuck are you looking like that for? Oh, what? You thought I was getting some liquor, didn't you? You stay with that fuck shit. What, I can't get something other than alcohol?"

Keyshia said. The tone of her voice was very aggressive, and she was on defense-mode.

Joy was shocked, and she didn't even know how to respond. Clearly something was wrong with Keyshia. What pissed Joy off was the fact that she invited her to lunch and she seemed annoyed.

"Look, I don't know what's wrong with you, but if you knew you weren't in the mood to be bothered, you should've never invited me to lunch. So what you want to do?" Joy asked Keyshia, pretty much letting her know they could leave.

"Whatever, Joy. Let's just order," Keyshia replied.

The waiter came back to the table and took their order. Once he left, there was an awkward silence for a few, and then Joy broke the silence. "So what's been up, chick? You've been missing from the scene since we got back. What's good?" Joy asked and took a sip of her drink.

Keyshia took a deep breath. She wanted badly to tell her friend that she was pregnant and didn't know who the father of her child was because she was raped by more than one dude. Keyshia really didn't want to get into all that, and she knew Joy would say to call the police and all that other shit. Besides, Keyshia had no clue who they were, and she didn't plan on keeping the baby anyways. She wanted kids but not like that. All this was never coming out. So she just lied.

"Nothing really. I've just been swamped at work. These people are killing me. I am so tired sometimes, I forget what day it is. So I've just been chilling," Keyshia told her.

"I feel you. I've been a bit overwhelmed myself with all this divorce drama and shit. But I try to do things to keep myself focused because I have to make sure I'm on my shit, so I can continue to be there for my daughter. It's really tough," Joy said to Keyshia as she fidgeted with her fingers. She, too, had a lot on her mind and had things she held deep inside. It was tearing her apart, but this shit was too deep to ever come to light. They both trusted each other and had shared secrets before, but this was just too much. So they chatted for a little while longer and then left.

After Keyshia dropped Joy home, she headed to her doctor's appointment to get the results from all the other testing she had done. It had been a while since she had been to the doctor, and plus, she wanted to be sure the home pregnancy test was right. Not that she was planning to keep the baby—she just wanted to be sure, and she wanted to get other testing done to make sure everything else was okay. After waiting for about thirty minutes, it was time for her to see the doctor. As she was getting up, she could feel butterflies in her stomach. She was extremely nervous. Keyshia didn't know what to expect. Once she got in the room, the doctor told her to have a seat. She sat down, and she noticed that there was someone else in the room. That made her really freak out.

"Doctor Hammons, what's going on? Why is someone else in the room?" Keyshia asked the doctor. You could hear the fear in her voice as she was hesitant to sit down.

"Have a seat, Mrs. Daniels," the doctor instructed Keyshia as he motioned towards the chair. She knew something had to be seriously wrong because he never called her by her last name.

Part of Keyshia wanted to just walk out and leave. Her heart really couldn't take what she was about to hear. She decided to go through this alone, and that made it harder. She really didn't know what to expect, but she was ready to hear it, so she sat down. "Lord, please let it don't be anything serious," she mumbled to herself. "Okay, Dr. Hammons, what's going on? Am I pregnant, or was the test I took wrong? I hope the test was wrong," Keyshia said to the doctor. You could hear it in her voice how anxious and scared she was at the same time.

Dr. Hammons was nervous himself. It was never a pleasure for him to have to give news like this. "Well, Keyshia, before we get to that, let me introduce you to Bethany Jones. Bethany is our counselor here at the office. She normally assists us with giving patients counseling on certain life changes and helps them get any extra assistance they may need," Dr. Hammons explained to Keyshia. Then Bethany leaned forward to shake her hand. Keyshia shook her hand.

"Nice to meet you. But, Doc, you know I already told you that if I am pregnant, I'm not keeping the baby. So I appreciate your offer and the assistance that you all provide, but there is no way I'm changing my mind," Keyshia told the doctor in a firm tone. By the look on her face, you could tell she was dead-ass serious, and her mind was set.

Dr. Hammons could see how serious she was, so he decided to explain more to Keyshia. "Ms. Daniels…"

Keyshia cut him off. "Please call me Keyshia."

"Okay, Keyshia, I really don't know a better way to say this. Yes, you are pregnant. You are about a little more than four weeks," the doctor told her. Then he paused for a moment.

"Okay, that seems about correct, so when can we handle business to get rid of it?" Keyshia bluntly said to him.

"Before we go that far, I'm so sorry to say that according to all your other testing, you have the HIV virus. I'm…"

Before he could finish, Keyshia just began to scream as loud as she could. "No! Oh Lord, please tell me there is a mistake! Dr. Hammons, are you fucking sure? Maybe your lab fucked up with the results. There is no fucking way. Please don't do this to me. No, please. Why me?" Keyshia continued to say. She fell from the chair on to the floor and just cried and asked why this had happened to her. Deep inside she knew the life she was living could lead to something like this, but she thought she was careful.

Dr. Hammons and Bethany tried to get her off the floor. They understood that this was news no one wanted to hear. "Keyshia, I can understand what may be going through your head, but we are going to help," Bethany said. She was trying to give Keyshia some reassurance or a positive side of the situation, but that pissed Keyshia off. She rose up from the floor and charged at Bethany. She grabbed her and slung her to the floor with her hands round her neck.

"Bitch! Help me how? Tell me how in the fuck can you help me? Are you going to make it disappear? Huh? What the fuck can you do?" Keyshia yelled as she kept her hands round her neck.

Dr. Hammons tried pulling her off Bethany. "Keyshia, let her go. Please let go," he said. Then he yanked her off Bethany, grabbed her in his arms, and held her while she cried. Her tears seemed never-ending. You could feel the pain she had inside by the way she sobbed and cried. For about another thirty minutes or so, Dr. Hammons sat on the floor holding Keyshia as she cried and asked, "Why did this happen to me?"

Dr. Hammons wasn't really this close with all his patients the way he was with Keyshia. This was probably because Keyshia was the only patient of his that he had ever slept with. Yes, Keyshia and him had had a sexual relationship a while back during the time he was going through his divorce. But thanks to the good Dr. Cheryl, Dr. Hammons and his wife had decided to give their marriage another try. That's when he decided to end things with Keyshia. Their relationship was strictly sex, so it didn't bother either of them for her to continue coming to his office. He, too, knew Keyshia was wild, and he also tried to tell her to slow down. But Keyshia blew him off just as she did everyone else. She felt she had one life to live, so she was going to live it however she pleased. And that's exactly what she did, not knowing or ever expecting a thing like this would come. She finally came up for air from crying. Her eyes were bloodshot red. So many questions and thoughts ran through her head, and she didn't know where to begin. The room got quiet, and the silence was awkward, so Bethany decided to break the ice. She was not mad at all at Keyshia for her reaction to the news. She didn't know Keyshia or her lifestyle, so she felt bad for her.

"Keyshia, I understand your pain and the reason you reacted the way that you did. This is tough news on anyone, and I know it will not be easy to handle. That's why we are here to help you," Bethany explained to Keyshia, but she really wasn't trying to hear that.

"Help me how? You all have a cure? Well, if that's the case, I have nothing to worry about, right?" Keyshia asked in a sarcastic tone. Neither of them responded to Keyshia, so she responded for them. "No! Exactly what the fuck I thought!" she yelled, and tears began to fall down her face. She got quiet again and just sat there crying. Bethany knew it was hard, but they needed to speak with her so they could try to find the source. Keyshia also needed to warn her partner, if there was one.

"Like I said, Keyshia, I understand your pain. I honestly do," Bethany continued "And of course, what we are sitting here saying is not really the help you are looking for. However, it can help you get through this. There is no cure, and yes, this is something that can kill you. But how longer you will live is determined by you and how you let this affect you. It's a huge change in your life right now, and there are so many questions you want answered. There are so many things you do not understand, and you want them to be explained to you, and that's the help we are going to provide. We will assist you with adjusting and understanding this change in your life." Bethany paused and walked towards Keyshia to try to comfort her. Keyshia didn't resist; she fell in Bethany's arms and cried like a little child.

For about another hour or so, Dr. Hammons and Bethany explained things to her and told her about the assistance she could get. In the conversation, the question was brought up again. "Do you know who you could have contracted this from? Was it the father of your child?"

Keyshia was never the type to be ashamed of the life she lived or how she did things. Her motto was always, "Fuck what people have to say. Bitches talk whether you doing good or bad." That same attitude was what had gotten her in the mess she was in now. At this moment when Bethany asked who could it be, she felt some kind of way. Keyshia didn't know how to respond, but then she thought, *Fuck it. What's the worst that can happen?* So she decided to just be straight-up although Dr. Hammons was there, and he didn't know all about her. Part of her was afraid of what he would think, but shit, it was forever ago when they were fucking around, and it only happened a few times before he ended it. They always used protection because he still didn't know what he wanted to do with his marriage at the time, so their relationship was a bit more emotional than physical, come to think of it. But she thought to herself, *What if he is worried that he got it, too?*

He wasn't worried at all; he knew his status, and they used protection, so he wasn't worried. Keyshia sat there for a moment still thinking. Besides the rape, who could have done this to her?

"Look, I have always been careful. How could this have happened?" she said to herself out loud.

"That's what we have to try and figure out."

Keyshia sat and thought long and hard, and then it hit her. "There's only one guy I have been having unprotected sex with on a regular basis for over a year now," Keyshia told them. "But

I really prefer not to give you all his info just yet," she said. "So could it have been from him?" she asked.

"Well, that is a possibility, and that's something we have to look into. Is he the father of this baby?" Bethany asked.

Keyshia let out a long sigh before she answered. "No! He and I have not seen each other in about two months or so. The father of this child is unknown," she stated. Then tears ran down her face as that night replayed in her head. She wiped her face and began to tell the story. "I was out on vacation last month with my friends and…" She paused in between her sentence and sniffled. "One night while we were out at this club, I ended up meeting this dude. I was a bit tipsy and decided to leave with him." She paused again, and the tears fell harder this time.

By the look on her face, Dr. Hammons and Bethany could tell what she was going to say next. They didn't interrupt; they allowed her to take her time to finish. She continued, "Once we got to his hotel room, we sat and chilled for a few and we had a few more drinks. We started kissing, and he was feeling all over me, and one thing led to another, and we started fucking. He had finished, and then whispered in my ear and said, 'Baby, don't be stingy. Let my boys get some.' I tried getting up and told him to get the fuck off me. It wasn't that type of party. He told me to shut the fuck up and said I decided to come get fucked, so that's exactly what I was going to do." Keyshia stopped talking and just kept crying; she couldn't even finish the story. The thought of that night burned her inside. It really hurt. She felt so nasty and just like a piece of nothing. Talking about it only made her feel worse, so instead of going through more details of it, she just got straight to the point.

"To get straight to the point, three other dudes fucked me while I was pinned down, and two of them didn't even use a fucking condom!" Keyshia yelled. She sat there and just cried.

Both Dr. Hammons and Bethany were speechless. Dr. Hammons felt some kind of way but didn't say much. Keyshia could sense their emotions by the way they had reacted. It really touched Bethany, and she knew exactly what Keyshia was feeling at that point. She had been gang-raped herself when she was teenager. In her case, the people who had raped her used protection, and she was only damaged emotionally. The thought of it still bothered her to this day. She looked at Keyshia and began to feel her pain.

"Keyshia, sweetheart, that's a terrible feeling, and this I know too well. All I can say is that with time and a strong support system, you will find a way to cope with this. I will not stand here and lie to you and say everything's going to be alright because, to be really honest, it's not. This is just the beginning of a long, hard battle you are about to fight, but one thing about this is that you don't have to fight it alone. We are here for you. I know what I'm saying doesn't mean anything to you right now, and you're angry, hurt, and confused, and that is understandable. Just give us a chance to help you. Don't give up like most people do," Bethany told Keyshia.

Keyshia sat and cried and listened to her. She really didn't know what to say. The only things that ran through her head were questions of how and why. She didn't know what to do.

She knew she would need a support system, but she really didn't want to tell her friends. So many things ran through her head. She knew what she was about to ask was a long-shot, but she asked anyways.

"So, Doc, do you think it was one of the guys who raped me?"

Dr. Hammons figured she would ask that question, and he was prepared to answer it. "I figured you would ask that. After reviewing your results, it seems you've had this for a while." Dr. Hammons's voice cracked when he began asking her the questions. "Besides the rape, are those the only people you can think of with whom you've had unprotected sex?" he asked and then looked at Keyshia, waiting for her response.

Keyshia dropped her head low and sniffled. She just didn't want to believe any of this was true or actually happening to her. She lifted her head up and wiped her eyes. "Like I said before, there was only one guy I had unprotected sex with on a regular basis, and I haven't fucked him in a while. So other than that, no," Keyshia said. You could tell by the tone in her voice she was upset. "Look, let's just do something about this fucking baby, and all the other shit we can deal with later. I really still can't believe this shit is happening to me. Oh my god, what the fuck!" Keyshia yelled. Then she got up and started pacing the floor.

Dr. Hammons and Bethany didn't say anything. They knew that trying to get her to understand right now wasn't going to work. Because Dr. Hammons knew her, this was going to be more painful for him to deal with than it normally was. Bethany could pick up that he felt something for Keyshia, so she just followed his lead. After a few more minutes, they were able to calm Keyshia down. They talked to her little more and gave her information about what she would go through. Bethany wanted to be sure that Keyshia really wanted to get rid of the baby, so she asked her one last time.

"Keyshia, I know what you said, but I just want to be sure you're not making a decision out of anger. We do have treatment and programs that can help you with the baby."

Before Bethany could finish, Keyshia cut her off. "This is the last fucking time I'm going to say this. No, I don't want to keep this fucking baby. My mind was made up way before I got the other results. So let's just do this, and stop asking me if I want to fucking keep it. Are we done with all these fucking questions? This shit is getting on my nerves," she said.

Dr. Hammons gave her some information, a prescription, and a few appointment dates to come back. Bethany gave Keyshia her number and some numbers to a few support groups. Keyshia took the information from them and left the office. Dr. Hammons was still a bit shocked and not sure how to feel. He told the assistant to tell his next patient to give him a few minutes. Then he went into his office restroom and stood and stared in the mirror. All types of thoughts ran through his head. He knew that he was okay because he had just recently taken an exam. Plus, it had been ages since he and Keyshia slept together, and they had used protection. Even so, it made him think, *damn that could've been me. I could've given it to my wife. Fuck, I'm lucky.* He stood there for a moment. Then he washed his hands and face, got himself together, and headed out to see his next patient for the day.

Keyshia made it home. She sat in her living room on the couch and just cried. So much ran through her head, and she didn't know what to do or who to turn to. Even the thought of killing herself ran across her mind. She knew that keeping it inside would only bother her more, but she didn't want anyone finding out her secret and judging her. "Lord, what do I do? Please, God, help me," she cried out. Over the next two hours or so, she sat on the couch and cried till she eventually fell asleep.

A few days had gone by, and no one had heard from Keyshia. She even had taken a leave of absence from work. Every time Joy or Cheryl would call her, she either sent them to voicemail or lied and said she was still out of town visiting some relatives and she would call them when she got back. She had the abortion and started taking the medication. She still hadn't thought of any solution or figured out how she was going to deal with this or live like this. She didn't attend any of the support groups in person. She called the hotline from time to time just to talk to someone when she felt alone. It was anonymous, so she didn't have to worry about anyone knowing. Although talking to the counselors seemed to help for the moment, Keyshia still felt some kind of way. She really missed her friends and family, but she didn't want to reveal her deep secret. Not only would it have people talking, but it could really hurt other people and change their lives. She knew she had to tell them. Part of her felt guilty for not telling them, and the guilt was eating away at her. She had to find a way to escape the feelings she was feeling. She needed a way to let it out to the ones who loved her. So Keyshia decided to write a letter.

"Dear Bitches," she began…

Chapter Eleven

CHERYL HAD BEEN BACK AND forth out of town for the past few weeks, and she and Chuck were still patching things up. She barely saw or talked to her friends. Since today she only had to meet one client in the office and chat with a few people, she decided to call Joy to see what was up before her appointment.

"Hey, boo, what's popping?" Joy greeted her as she answered the phone in a cheerful voice. You could tell she was excited to hear from her girl.

"Hey! You sound so excited to hear from me. I miss you. What's been up?" Cheryl responded.

"I missed you, too, and yes I'm excited to hear from at least one of my best friends. What's been going on? How's work and the family?" Joy asked her.

"Everything is finally starting to settle down. The kids are good. Business has been busy. What about you?"

"I've been chilling. I postponed on opening up another location. Thank God my divorce is final, and Paul has got the picture that there is no turning back. This nigga thought I was going to be the mistress after being his wife all those years," Joy told her and started laughing. "But everything is cool. When are we going to link up? It's well overdue. And have you heard from Kesh? It's been a while since I saw her. This is not like her. I hope she's okay," Joy said in a concerned voice. It was normal for Cheryl to be gone a lot due to the business trips and stuff, but not Keyshia. She was always around, so it really worried Joy.

"No, I was going to ask you about that. I mean, I called her a couple of weeks ago, and she said she was visiting some family and that she would call me back once she go back in town. But she never called, and when I call, she brushes me off. So I haven't called or heard from her. I hope she's okay, too," Cheryl told Joy.

"Yeah, same here. I guess she will come around. She said she's okay, so I guess we will wait for her to reach out to us. But when are we going to meet up, chick?" Joy asked Cheryl.

Cheryl looked down at her schedule to see when she would be free. "Do you want to do lunch tomorrow or a night out?" she asked Joy.

"I prefer a night out. Are you free for dinner tomorrow night?" Joy responded. She wanted to do dinner because an hour-long lunch wouldn't be enough time to catch up and tell her friend what's been really going on in her life. As Cheryl got ready to tell her yes, her other line beeped. She checked the caller ID, and it read, "Unknown," so she ignored it.

"Sure, that would be great. How does nine sound?"

"That's perfect. Let's go to Joe's!" Joy said. She loved that damn place.

Cheryl shook her head. She wanted to say no and pick somewhere else, but she hadn't seen her friend in a while, so she agreed. "That's a shame. You never get tired of that place, but okay, I will see you tomorrow at nine," Cheryl said. Then they said their goodbyes, and Cheryl prepared for her client.

As soon as she hung up with Joy, her phone rang. Once again it was an unknown number. This time she decided to answer it. "Hello, this is Cheryl. May I ask who's speaking?" she said in the phone.

"Yes, you may. It's your boo," the male voice on the other end said. Cheryl recognized the voice and began to smile. It was Morris's sexy ass. She shook her head. She knew she said she wouldn't talk to him after the sexual incident in her office, but she couldn't resist the feeling he gave her when they were with each other. Yes, with each other.

After their sexing in her office, Cheryl ran into Morris a week later at a conference she attended at the Miami Beach Convention. The first thing Morris said to her when he saw that day was, "Fate." All she could do was smile. So after the convention was over, they went and had a few drinks. They ended up in his hotel room fucking. It was amazing, and it made Cheryl feel some kind of way. Yeah, it was wrong because she was married, and she tried to keep people from doing the very same thing she was doing, but it was a bit too late to follow her own advice now. Since the convention, Cheryl and Morris had seen each other every chance they got, and each time was better than the last. It excited her when she saw or heard from him, and it showed. The feeling was mutual. Hearing his voice made her melt, and his dick would jump just by the tone of her voice. "What's up, Mister? I thought we had an agreement," Cheryl said to Morris in a soft tone. Morris grabbed his dick and smiled because he knew he wasn't supposed to be calling her. He couldn't help it; hearing her voice always made his day.

"Damn, baby, I know, but I just had to hear that sexy-ass voice. When am I going to see you again, Mrs. Lady?" Morris said to her.

Cheryl chuckled because they had just seen each other. Of course she wanted to see him really bad, but they agreed not to see each other so often and mainly to see each other when they went on business trips. She didn't want either of their spouses to become suspicious. Morris wasn't trying to hear that. Besides, his wife already accused him of cheating way before he and Cheryl met. He felt it was whatever, but Cheryl still wanted to be careful.

"Now, you know what we agreed to. Besides, I'm busy today, and Chuck and I have dinner plans later," Cheryl told Morris. Her tone was soft and sexy. She wasn't trying to turn him on or anything. She just didn't want her assistant to hear her conversation with Morris, but Morris didn't care about any of that.

"Well, just cancel your plans with him. Tell him it's an emergency or something," Morris told Cheryl she began to laugh. She found it really humorous, but little did she know, he was dead serious.

"What's so funny? Is someone there making you laugh?"

"No one is here making me laugh. I'm laughing at what you said. Sweetie, you know I can't cancel, but we will see each other real soon," Cheryl told him.

Morris wasn't too pleased with Cheryl's response, but he understood. He knew the last time he tried to pull something like this, she told him she would call the whole thing off, and he didn't want to jeopardize his being able to see or touch Cheryl. So he went with the flow for the moment.

"Okay, baby, I understand. I guess I will wait till our time."

"Yes, and you know what they say, Mister," Cheryl replied.

"No I don't. What do they say, love?" Morris asked Cheryl in a somewhat sarcastic tone.

"They say good things come to those who wait," Cheryl told him and then giggled.

That made Morris smile. All types of freaky thoughts ran through his mind. Instead of telling her his freaky thoughts like he always did, he just agreed. "You are so right about that. Good things sure do come to those wait, so I will be patiently waiting, baby," Morris said.

For about twenty more minutes, he and Cheryl laughed and chatted on the phone. Besides their sexual attraction to each other, Cheryl and Morris actually had a lot in common, and that made the situation even harder. They finally said their goodbyes. After hanging up with Morris, Cheryl got prepared for her appointment. This client who was coming was something else, both she and her husband. Cheryl really didn't understand what went on in their brains. The shit they had going on as a married couple was just ridiculous. But like always, Cheryl just voiced her opinion and gave them suggestions. Most of her clients would listen and at least attempt to try something Cheryl told them, but not these two—not at all. They both seemed to think what they had going was perfect. If they felt that way, why in the fuck did they come to her for help? It puzzled her. Her thoughts were interrupted when her assistant buzzed her phone to let her know her client was there.

"Okay, thanks. Send them in, and can you grab me a water?" Cheryl told her assistant. A few minutes later, her client came in her office. Cheryl greeted her. "Hi, Maxine. How are you? It's good to see you again." Cheryl shook her client's hand and motioned for her to take a seat.

"I'm doing okay, I guess," Maxine replied, although Cheryl could tell by the tone in her voice she wasn't doing okay. Cheryl planned on finding out what had gone wrong. Cheryl noticed that Maxine's husband Malcom was not with her.

"Will Malcolm be joining us today?" she asked.

"No, it's just me. I really needed to see you alone. So much has changed since the last time I saw you, and when I say changed, I mean it's changed," Maxine told Cheryl with a nonchalant look on her face.

Cheryl was used to that look. Maxine always seemed to have no emotions; no matter what, her attitude remained the same. Cheryl would always ask her if she really cared about anything. Maxine would giggle and say yes, but Cheryl didn't know whether to believe her or not. See, Maxine and her husband had started coming to Cheryl a few months ago. Maxine and Malcolm were married. Malcolm is still in love with his ex, but he couldn't leave Maxine because she was the love of his life. At one point, Maxine agreed to him still seeing his ex, but then he started sneaking around, buying gifts, and spending nights and vacations with her. That pissed Maxine off; it was one thing that he still loved this ho, but to be treating her like she was the one with ring was another. So they ended up coming to an agreement where Malcolm was free to see his ex. He could fuck her but nothing more. And since Maxine loved women, he agreed to let her play alone with women. Normally they would both enjoy the body of another woman, but since he couldn't stop seeing his ex, they came to it that Maxine could step out with women only. Oh yes, that's exactly what she did. She would go out nights and have foursomes with women. It really excited her, especially just tasting the sweet, wet juices of another woman's pussy. And to Malcolm's knowledge, all Maxine was doing was fucking women. But then he found out she had joined a swingers' club and was a preferred member at that. It pissed him off, so that's when they came to see Cheryl. Every session Maxine found it so amusing that Malcolm was pissed. She felt that it was his idea, so he had to deal with it, but he said he had agreed to her seeing women, not men and women. So after a few sessions Malcolm agreed to leave his ex-girlfriend alone and work on the marriage just the two of them. However, Maxine was having too much fun; she didn't want to stop. So she told him she would stop going to the swingers' club and he can keep his ex, but she was still going to do her. Malcolm didn't want that, and Cheryl tried to warn Maxine that nothing good would come from this, but you couldn't tell her that. Her being at Cheryl's office could only mean one thing; Shit had gotten real.

"Changed how? Last I heard from you or Malcolm, things were okay," Cheryl said to her and grabbed her note pad.

"Yes, they were. At least that's what I thought until I found out I'm pregnant," Maxine said and looked away. You could tell she was fighting back tears, and this was not like her. Maxine was never really emotional, and Cheryl didn't know what to say.

"Wow! That's great, isn't it? I thought..." Cheryl couldn't finish because Maxine cut her off.

"What the hell do you mean great? No, this isn't great at all. Malcolm wants to leave me because he doesn't think it's his."

"Why is that? Please don't tell me you're still out there 'playing around,' as you call it. Maxine, I thought you said you would cut that out. And to be doing it unprotected! You know the health risk you put yourself and Malcolm at. So what do you plan to do?" Cheryl said to her. She couldn't believe how careless Maxine had been. She never really understood why either of them wanted to continue this stupid game. Marriage was supposed to be sacred. Cheryl always told people, "If it makes you happy, go for it, but be prepared for the consequences."

"I really don't know what to do. Malcolm won't talk to me, and now he is talking about divorce. What have I done? I never thought it would go this far. Tell me how to fix it, Cheryl!"

For the first time, Cheryl saw Maxine shed tears. She started crying and couldn't stop. She was actually hurt. Cheryl was speechless because part of her really didn't think Maxine cared. Now, as she was about to lose it all, her true emotions were showing.

"If you are sincere, fight for your marriage. Show him these emotions that you are showing me now. You have to be submissive to him, but you have to be doing it because of the love and not just because you feel you have to battle. If you truly want this marriage to work, both of you have to make a sacrifice and stop these games. Seriously!" Cheryl told Maxine.

She had stopped crying, and she knew that some of what Cheryl was saying was right. She was willing to do it, but she was afraid Malcolm wouldn't be willing to. See, once he found out about the pregnancy, he swore if it wasn't his, it was over—and Maxine wasn't sure who the father was.

"Yes, I want it to work, and I'm willing to make the sacrifice, but I'm not sure if this is Malcolm's baby. Better yet, I think I am pretty sure it's not. There is no working anything out."

Damn, shit was really crazy! "Well, what are you prepare to do?" Cheryl asked.

"I may have to lose my husband, the love of my life. Shit, I fucked up really bad."

"No matter the outcome, I'm going to help you through this. We will find a way. It sucks, but it's just a lesson learned."

They talked for a little while more, and Cheryl told her she would check on her in a few days. She told her she would call Malcolm and try to see if she could talk to him and see where his head was really at. Maxine thanked her and then left. Cheryl sat there and just shook her head. She knew something would go wrong, but damn. She hoped they could work through it, but she knew that if it wasn't Malcolm's baby, there was no hope for that. "Damn," Cheryl said to herself. She took a few moments to jot down some notes and get prepared for her appointment with Nadine.

Chapter Twelve

SHE HADN'T SEEN NADINE IN a while, but they had been speaking with each other via e-mail and phone. Nadine said she needed to see her, and that was cool with Cheryl. After she finished up her notes, Nadine walked into her office. She looked happier than the last time Cheryl saw her, which made Cheryl believe everything was going well, but she wouldn't know for sure until they started talking. Nadine took a seat after they greeted each other, and then they got to talking.

"It's been a while since I last saw you, and I must say you are looking amazing. Is it safe to assume things are getting better at home?" Cheryl said to Nadine.

"Well, thank you, and yes, it's been a while. However, I won't go so far as to say things have gotten better. Let's just say it's all a mystery," Nadine responded to Cheryl and let out a chuckle.

Cheryl laughed with her and then took a sip of her water. "Well, what's been going on? I know the last time we spoke, you said he was on a business trip, but when you tried reaching out to him, there was no contact. And I thought you said he would be coming to our next session," Cheryl said to Nadine with a somewhat puzzled look on her face. She thought things were getting a little better at least.

"Yes, you've got that right. I thought he would be coming. Shit, me and you both thought he would be coming," Nadine said and let out a long sigh. She was really getting tired of her husband's shit, and it was wearing thin. Cheryl could sense Nadine's frustration and could tell she was at her breaking point. Cheryl wanted to help her, but she just didn't know how. So far Nadine had no hardcore evidence that her husband really was doing anything; he was just always missing. Cheryl was determined to figure something out.

For a moment there was an awkward silence, then Cheryl started talking. "Well, why is it that he didn't join us today? Is he away on another business trip or something?" she asked.

"No, his ass is actually in town. He just keeps saying he doesn't see the purpose in us both going and that he has talked to someone. So if I want to continue to come spend money for no reason, I can go ahead," Nadine told Cheryl. Tears began to fill Nadine's eyes. She wiped her face, held them back, and finished talking. "It's like I really don't know what to do or say anymore. I know relationships have to be built on trust, or they won't work, but shit just doesn't seem right. I've tried a few of the things you told me, and sometimes they work for a moment and things are good with us, but then shit just goes sour. Now it's affecting our sex life, so I'm more than sure that he's fucking around. It's just a matter of time before he really slips, and when he does, I hope like hell he is prepared for what I have to offer," Nadine said. She stood and walked over to the window. As she stood there staring out at the view, tears ran down her face.

Cheryl got up and handed her some tissues. She never told any of her clients not to cry; she would allow them to cry. She always said it was part of getting it all out. They were silent again for a moment as Nadine cried. Cheryl didn't want to seem like she was rushing her, but she had a busy day, so she got on with the session.

"When you say it's affecting your sex life, what do you mean? And how?" Cheryl asked Nadine. She grabbed her pen and note pad to take notes. Nadine walked away from the window and sat on the loveseat. She wiped her eyes once more and started talking.

"Well before when he would come back from a business trip after being gone for a few days, he would surprise me and come back earlier than the time he told me. And when I got home, he would be waiting for me with either a gift or just lying naked on the bed with his dick rock hard, and we would fuck for hours. He would fuck me like it was our first time. First that stopped, and I brushed it off. I just figured maybe the routine was getting old although I didn't mind it because each time we did it, it got better and better," Nadine said with a slight smile on her face. You could tell the memories made her feel some kind of way.

"Okay, so you said maybe the routine got old, which can happen at times. So let me ask you, have you tried other things, or have you tried surprising him instead?"

"Yes. That's the problem. When I noticed he wasn't doing the usual anymore, I thought, *Well maybe he wants me to surprise him*. So when he got home, I had the bath running for him and dinner cooked and warm. I even sucked his dick at the table while he ate his dinner. It worked for a little while. We had great sex. Then shit stopped. Each time he went away and came back, he claimed he was too tired or too busy to even have sex with his fucking wife. And the only time we would fuck was if I keep bitching about it. Then he would fuck me, but he would fuck me like I'm a fucking sideline bitch or something. It's really getting on my freaking nerves," Nadine told Cheryl.

"I could understand how its making you feel. You seem like you're at your breaking point. What do you want to do, or what have you tried doing?" Cheryl asked Nadine.

Nadine had a puzzled look on her face because part of her wanted to call it quits, but something was keeping her there. "I want to stay, but I also want to go. I love my husband. I feel there is no other man for me. We have so much history. How could we be at this point? What am I doing wrong? I don't cheat; I cook; I clean; I'm loyal; I make sure he is treated like a king. What is it? I've done everything you've suggested. I just don't know," Nadine said, and the tears ran down her cheeks again.

Cheryl felt her pain, and she knew what she was about to say. Nadine probably didn't want to hear it, but hey, it was her job. "Listen, Nadine, nobody's perfect, but don't think that it's all your fault. No matter how good you are to a person, if they want to leave or cheat, they will do it regardless. And if you feel there is something wrong or you know you're not being treated right, don't hold on in fear. See, a huge part of you is tired of being neglected, and you feel like you're in this marriage alone, and you want out. But then there's the other part that wants to stay because he is all you know and you are afraid of starting over.

Yes, I know starting over is hard, but you have to really know and be sure about what you want. See, he continues to play this game because he knows you. He knows you will talk shit, but you're not about to leave."

"You have a point, and yes, I am scared, but he doesn't know me. He doesn't know what I am capable of," Nadine responded to Cheryl.

"Let me ask you this. So let's say you catch him in the act; are you going to leave him?" Cheryl asked her.

Nadine sat there and didn't say a word. She didn't expect that curve ball. She talked the talk but never felt she should have to live up to it. Cheryl figured she couldn't answer that question at the moment. So they chatted a bit more, and Nadine expressed some more emotions. Cheryl suggested Nadine get more facts and really think about the choice she wanted to make. No matter what, in the end she had to live with it and be happy with what she chose. Once they finished talking, she scheduled to hear from her in a week. As Nadine was walking out the door, Cheryl stopped her and said, "Remember, things always get worse before they get better. Whatever happens, it happened for a reason. Be careful, and I'm here anytime you need me." They hugged, and Nadine left. When Nadine left the office she made a stop by the mall. She grabbed a few things and headed home.

To her surprise, when she pulled up her husband's car was there. She was surprised to see him home. Nadine was nervous; she was expecting to walk in and catch him with someone or something because he was supposed to be busy. So she took a deep breath, got out of the car, and headed inside. When she opened the door, there were rose petals from the start of the door leading to the living room. When Nadine made it all the way into the living room, her face lit up. She saw rose petals all over the living room, and her favorite flowers, tulips, filled every inch of the room. On the ottoman she saw the biggest bunch of tulips and a note attached to it. Nadine was shocked, excited, and nervous all at the same time. She grabbed the note and read it. "Hey, baby. I know things have not been so good between us, and my attitude and my working so much are not making it easier. So tonight is your night. Follow the petals, and let your man take care of you. Love you."

Nadine was smiling so hard her cheeks were hurting. She followed her husband's instructions, and when she reached her destination, she was in tears of joy. He had their master suite looking like a five-star hotel spa. He had even hired a masseuse to give her a massage. After being pampered, Nadine was given a full bath by hand from her husband. Then he dried her off and lotioned her entire body, and he laid her down on the bed and kissed and licked every inch of her brown, sexy, smooth frame. Nadine was in heaven. For the next three hours, they made love to each other till they both fell asleep.

That next morning, Nadine woke up to breakfast waiting for her and a note from her husband. "Last night was magical. Sorry I had to leave so early. I'll see you later. Love your boo, forever." Nadine smiled, ate her breakfast, and then got dressed and ready for her day.

Chapter Thirteen

"DAMN, I'M SO TIRED I could lie here with you all day," John told Joy and then kissed her on the lips. Joy smiled as she was enjoying the moment also, but she knew John had to leave, and she needed to get her day started.

"Yes, wouldn't that be nice? But we both know that can't happen," she told him. He sucked his teeth and pouted like a child.

"Why are we still sneaking around, Joy? I understand keeping it a secret in the beginning, but shit, we're both are single. Finally, your year-long divorce is over, so there is no reason we can't be together publicly," John said to Joy as he got up out of the bed and began to get dressed. Joy could sense his attitude and knew that this time he was serious. He would normally talk shit like this every so often, but she paid it no mind because he had known the situation since they started this. She didn't like keeping it a secret, but it was best that way.

"Look, it's just not the right timing. I'm sure you can understand that, and besides..."

Before Joy could get another word out, he cut her off. This time she could feel his anger. "What the fuck do you mean, 'It's not the right time?' We've been doing the same secret-lovers shit for like two years. Now at first I dealt with it 'cause of your marriage. You're finally divorced although shit, you should've been divorced long time ago. So this is my last time tell you this shit, Joy. If we have to keep sneaking and creeping, this shit we've got going is fucking over!"

Joy was speechless; she just sat on the bed quietly in a state of shock and watched him get dressed. She understood where he was coming from, but she had never expected them to last this long or for feelings to get so deep. She didn't know what to do. "John, look. I understand, but this shit is complicated to explain to people."

"What the fuck do we have to explain to any fucking body? Oh, I get it you don't want people to think of you a certain kind a way. You want to keep your squeaky-clean image. News flash, baby, you're just like the rest of us: fucked up. And that's just a part of life, so you need to figure out what you want to do because men like me don't come around too often. Don't let a good thing slip away from you because you're afraid of being judged. People judge you no matter what," John said to Joy and gave her a serious look. They were just standing there staring at each other; you could feel the tension in the room. Joy was a bit upset because she felt she was being pressured, and a part of her felt bad, but she had a lot at stake. She could not jeopardize losing her child or her business. Although she was happy with John and he treated her well, no one knew about them. Everyone thought Joy was still single and stuck on Paul, but that wasn't the case. Paul and Joy had been over for a while although the divorce took a year because Paul was on some bullshit.

Joy wanted it to be over, so she could be with John, but now that it was over, she was still afraid to let the secret out that she'd been sleeping with and having a relationship with her ex-husband's brother. Yes, she was fucking her brother-in-law. She didn't want to look like a trashy ho, but Paul was always out running around on her. In one of her moments when she needed someone to talk to, Cheryl was busy and Keyshia was out doing what Keyshia did. John came over to drop something off for Paul, not knowing Paul was not there. When Joy answered the door in tears, John came in and asked her what was wrong. He knew Paul had to have done something. John never understood why Joy stayed so long and endured all that emotional abuse from Paul, but he never said anything because he knew Paul would get pissed or say John was jealous. He always kept his comments to himself, but this time seeing Joy like that made him feel some kind of way. That night he consoled her, listened to her cry, and gave her more than just a shoulder to lean on. They made the sweetest love that night; he fucked her like she was the love of his life. From that day forward, they had been having this secret affair. John always complained about wanting to stop sneaking and creeping, but Joy would always make up some reason why they couldn't, and he would fall for it and drop the topic. But lately he had been getting restless and had even threatened Joy a few times that he would tell, but he never did. How he was talking now had Joy afraid. She felt this time he really might, so she had to come up with something.

"Wow! You've said a mouthful, John. It's not about being judged or anything like that. How the hell I tell my child that her uncle is now her step-dad? I couldn't give two fucks about what anyone else thinks; it's my child I'm concerned about. So tell me, since you want to talk all this bullshit, how do I explain this to my child?" Joy said to John. She tried to reverse things on him to take the heat off her, but this time, that shit didn't work. John was no fool.

"Look, honey, I'm not new to this shit you're trying to pull. I've written the book, read it, and rewritten it again. So this is just li'l fuck shit you're trying to pull to take the heat off yourself. You and I both know damn well that it's not only about your child. You don't want your friends or bitches or whatever the fuck you call them to know. cause if it wasn't about anyone else or what they would have to say, you would have at least told your therapist, your best friend. You confide in her about everything else, but I bet she knows nothing about this little secret. So fuck you with all that bullshit. I'm not debating about this shit anymore. Once you've figured out what you want to do, then you can holler at me. But don't think I'm going to sit around too long. I'm out yo." John told her. Then he grabbed his keys and left her standing there looking stupid.

Deep inside she knew John was right, but it was just too complicated. There was too much she would have to deal with and too many questions that would be asked. It was hard but also easier to keep it a secret. She cared deeply for John and didn't want to lose him, but damn, shit would get really ugly. She really needed to take some time to decide what she was going to do. She closed her eyes and let out a long sigh. Just as she was about to go shower and get dressed, her phone rang. She got a bit excited because she hoped it was John, but it was her aunt. "Are you serious? What the fuck could she want?" Joy said to herself. Instead of answering, she let it go to voicemail. Like always, her aunt left a message, but Joy didn't waste time to even listen to it because she knew what she would be saying. Instead she turned the phone off and got in the shower. As she let the water run on her body tears fell down her face. All she could so was replay the argument she and John had in her head. So many thoughts were running through her head, and she really didn't know what to do. She'd kept this secret for so long, she wouldn't know where to start to tell it. Joy had thought about telling Cheryl a few times, but she didn't know what to expect. She feared her friend judging her although she knew better than that; Cheryl was not like that at all. Besides, they'd known each other for years, and there had been so many secrets she had shared with Cheryl, and they stayed safe with her. But this was deep—too deep. "Lord, what do I do? What have I done?" Joy said to herself as she stood there naked, crying in the shower. Joy stood there for about a good forty-five minutes, crying and bathing her body. She finally got out of the shower and got dressed. She still hadn't decided on what to do. Instead of dwelling on it, she knew she had a busy day and wanted to make sure she got through with everything, so she would be ready to have dinner and drinks with Cheryl. Her plan was to tell Cheryl that she was seeing someone, but she wasn't going to tell her who it was just yet. She finished getting dressed. She stood there and smiled as she thought of how Cheryl and Keyshia would find it shocking that Joy was actually fucking someone. But if they only knew she been riding this dick for a while… Then she thought, *Damn where in the hell is Keyshia's ass? This is not like her.* She wanted her to be there. They'd had their ups and downs, but they were friends for life, and she really missed Keyshia. "I'm going to call this bitch, and she better answer, too," Joy said to herself out loud.

She turned on her phone. Once it finished loading up, she saw she had six voicemails. She looked and saw that four were from her aunt, one was from John, and one was from Cheryl. She listened to her aunt's message first. "Joy, pick up the damn phone! It's a fucking emergency!" her aunt yelled in the phone. That was the first message. Joy wasn't too convinced that it was an emergency, so she deleted it and listened to the next one her aunt had left.

"Joy, this is serious. Can you please cut this bullshit out and answer the fucking phone? It's a damn emergency!" her aunt yelled through the phone. Joy could hear in her voice that she just might be serious this time. Joy let out a long sigh before she began to call her aunt back. As she dialed her number and waited for her to answer, she mumbled to herself, "This bitch better have a real emergency." After about two rings, her aunt answered.

"Damn, Joy, why the hell wouldn't you answer the phone? Jeremy was in a car accident," her aunt said to her. You could hear that she was all out of breath. Joy's heart dropped. Jeremy was her younger brother, and she hadn't heard from him in forever. They stopped talking when he got mad because she wouldn't give him money. She didn't care that they were not on speaking terms, but she loved her brother, and the thought of something bad happening to him drove her crazy. She knew he lived a wild life. Her aunt finished giving her the details about what had happened, and just as Joy figured, Jeremy had done something wrong.

"You're telling me the he's okay, so what do you want with me?" Joy said to her aunt. She was pissed. Jeremy had been running from the police when he got into the wreck. He was alright, but he wanted Joy to come get him out of jail and give him money to head back home. He stayed in Atlanta, but he would come to Miami from time to time. Each time he came, he got into some shit. Joy wasn't in the mood for this shit her aunt and brother was trying to pull.

"Joy, this is your brother. Why do you have to be the way you are? I've told you time and time again, you never know when you're going to need some…"

Joy didn't even waste time arguing with her; she hung up the phone. She then called Cheryl back to see why she called. She hoped she wasn't cancelling their date because she really needed some good company. As soon as Cheryl answered, Joy didn't even give her a chance to speak.

"Please, bitch, don't tell me you called me to cancel our plans," Joy said to Cheryl. Cheryl couldn't do anything but laugh. She understood why Joy would think she was calling to cancel. She normally did, but this time she wasn't.

"First off, heifer, don't be doing me like that. I was actually calling to confirm if you were still able to go. Your aunt called and said Jeremy was in a car accident. Is he okay?" Cheryl said to her.

Joy sucked her teeth in frustration after hearing what Cheryl said. "Girl, her ass called me, too, with that bullshit. Now he's talking 'bout he needs some money and a way out of town. I don't have time for that bullshit. It never fails. It's always some shit with my family, and they are really getting on my nerves," Joy told Cheryl.

Cheryl knew how it was with Joy and her family, and she always told Joy she spoiled people too much, especially her family. "I know you, and you know what I always say, but thank god he's okay. So yes we're still on for tonight," Cheryl said. Joy chuckled and told her okay. They chatted a little more until Cheryl's other line beeped. She looked at the caller ID and saw it was Morris. This dude had been blowing her up, so she ignored it once again. Joy and Cheryl finally hung up, and Joy then decided to call John back. She didn't even listen to his message. After a few rings, he picked up. "Yeah?"

"Damn, that's how you answer the phone?" Joy said to him. She could tell in his voice that he was still pissed off from earlier, but she wasn't really in the mood for the bullshit.

"It's my phone. I answer it how the fuck I want to," John snapped back at her.

She didn't even respond; she just hung up. He called back, but she didn't answer. "He's got me fucked up. I ain't in the mood for this bullshit. Once he calms down, then maybe we could talk," Joy said to herself. She threw her phone down on the bed. A few minutes later, he texted her.

The message read, "Look, Joy, I don't know what type of fucking games you want to play, but I don't have time for this shit anymore. I'm a grown-ass man, and this creeping and secret shit is getting on my nerves. I love you, and you know that, but if we have to love in secret, then I would rather we just let this end before it gets any worse. So when you are ready to make up your mind, you know my number. Other than that, fuck it. Don't think I'm going to wait forever."

Joy stood there looking at the message in shock. She didn't know what to respond and say to him. Yeah, she understood how he felt, but this was a dirty secret that wouldn't come clean easily. She plopped down on the bed and let out a long sigh. This was too much to deal with, and she didn't know what to do. Joy finally shook herself out of it and went on with her day.

Later on, Cheryl and Joy met up at Joe's for dinner and drinks. They both arrived at the same time. "Hey, boo. What's up?" Joy greeted Cheryl, and they hugged each other and went inside. Once they were seated, the waiter asked if they wanted to order something to drink.

"Yes!" Joy said in an excited tone. Cheryl looked at her funny. She was used to Keyshia being ready to order something to drink. "Please make it the strongest drink you have. As a matter of fact, give me two of your strongest drinks," Joy told the waiter. Cheryl looked at the expression on her face and could tell something was wrong. She figured that was the reason Joy wanted to meet. So they both ordered their drinks, and Cheryl sat and waited for Joy to start talking. She never just jumped to asking questions, so Joy checked her phone and returned a text from Paul about their daughter. A few moments later, the waiter came back with the drinks and asked if they were ready to order their food. They ordered their food, and the waiter left again. Joy took a sip of her drink.

"Woo! Yes, now this is just what I needed!" she said and then sat her glass down. Cheryl was getting a bit restless waiting on Joy to say what was going on.

"What is up with you?" Cheryl asked Joy. She took a sip of her drink. Joy let out a long sigh. She still hadn't decided whether to tell Cheryl about her relationship with John or not.

"Girl, it's just been a long-ass week. I'm trying to decide whether to open up another store, and then my family is getting on my fucking nerves, as usual. Thank God the divorce is over after almost two years, but this motherfucker is calling me and talking 'bout how he's sorry and all this bullshit. It's all just so annoying," Joy told Cheryl. She picked up her drink and took a big gulp of it.

"Well, damn. Maybe you need a few more gulps of that drink," Cheryl said jokingly, and they both chuckled. Cheryl took a sip of her drink again and let out a long sigh. She was going through her own dilemma with this affair she was having with Morris, but there was no way she was telling Joy although she wanted so badly to tell her girl how he was dicking her down all the time. She was afraid of what her reaction would be, but not only that. Shit, she was supposed to be a role model for her clients and friends, so that wouldn't be a good look for her. But damn, it was killing her to keep this secret. She knew Joy wouldn't judge her, but then again you never know. She decided to continue to keep this affair of hers in the dark. Besides, she could tell by the look on Joy's face she had a lot on her mind, and Cheryl's natural instinct and job was to be there for her friend. She took a deep breath, cleared her throat, and put her considerate therapist's cap on.

"Joy, you know you are taking on way too much. I've told you time and time again you need to empty your plate. At least the divorce is finally over. I'm happy. You still have to deal with him for your daughter's sake, but besides that, fuck him," Cheryl told Joy. Joy let out a sigh. She agreed with Cheryl, and Paul really was the least of her worries. Yeah, his trifling ass was still trying to get back with her after all this shit. Part of her wanted to give him another chance, but his having a baby was a huge pill to swallow. A few times since the separation, Joy and Paul had fucked. Joy knew it wasn't right, but she didn't give a fuck. She never told Cheryl that she still was fucking Paul from time to time because she knew what she would say. To make matters worse, Joy was fucking Paul's brother and had been for about over a year. That was the shit that was eating her up inside. She wanted to ask Cheryl her opinion on what to do, but damn, she was afraid of what would happen. Her belief was always that secrets belonged in the dark, and it wasn't safe once they were in the light. Joy loved John, and she knew he loved her, but was the love they shared worth risking losing what she had? She shook her head and decided still not to tell Cheryl, at least not just yet. She decided to change the subject.

"Man, what's up with Keyshia? She still hasn't called me back. I called her job, and they said she took a leave of absence. I really hope she's okay," Joy said to Cheryl with a concerned and scared look on her face. This wasn't normal behavior for Keyshia, and it really made them worry.

"Girl, I know. This shit is really worrying me, and I don't even know her mom's number anymore. I called her cousin Michelle to see if she had heard from her, but she said no. I went by her place, and she wasn't there. This really isn't her. I wonder what's going on. Hopefully she's just going through one of her mood swings and doesn't want to be bothered. Let's just give her a li'l more time to come around," Cheryl told Joy. Joy shook her head and agreed with Cheryl. They stayed and ate and talked for a little while longer. Joy told her how the shop was coming along, and Cheryl told her the website was going well and how she was thinking of another business venture. One thing about Cheryl and Joy was that they both were very outgoing and always had different ideas and ways to get money. It was the hustle in them. Whether it worked or not, they would try it. So Cheryl told Joy more about her idea of a T-shirt line, and she wanted Joy to sell them in her boutiques. The idea she had was to use one of her poems she wrote and use some of the lines from the poem as slogans on the shirts. Cheryl wasn't just a therapist; she also loved to write, and she had written a few books. Some of them were full of relationship advice, and she also wrote a few poetry ones. So she was thinking of the idea one day and she did some research and since Joy owned her own clothing line and boutique she, figured there was no better person to go into business with. If they wanted to, they both could be famous, but fame was never something they desired to have. Just being able to enjoy life and support their families was enough. So Joy agreed. She was excited, and they discussed it a little more and decided on a date to meet up about it. After a few more drinks, they decided to call it a night. They said their goodbyes and went their separate ways.

When Cheryl reached her, car Morris called. Her face lit up when she saw his number. Everything in her told her not to answer because she had to get home to Chuck, but the tingling sensation she felt in her body just thinking of Morris made her answer. "Hello," she said into the phone.

"Hello, beautiful. I miss you so much!" Morris replied to her.

The sound of his voice made her heart skip a beat and her pussy jump. Damn, he sounded so fucking sexy.

"Oh, is that right?" Cheryl said to him with a smile on her face.

Morris could tell she was smiling by the sound in her voice, and he loved putting a smile on her face.

"It seems like you feel the same way," he said to her.

"And what makes you think I miss you, Mister?" Cheryl asked him jokingly.

"Baby girl, I can hear it all in your voice, and I know for a fact you miss me," Morris said and then laughed. He was always so cocky and confident in himself, and he had every right to be. It turned Cheryl on all the time when he talked like that. Yeah, he was cocky, but he could back it up, too. "So, my sexy lady, where have you been all day? I've been trying to reach you. I wanted to take you on a picnic, and then we could make a mess somewhere, baby," Morris told her.

By now Cheryl's pussy was dripping wet. Just the words "make a mess" coming out of his mouth made her have flashbacks of the first time he said they made a mess. Cheryl was soaking wet, so wet she left a puddle in the middle of the hotel bed. Morris loved playing in her pussy. He called it his wet puddle of pleasure. He left her laid on the middle of the bed with her legs spread open, and he sat there and played in that pussy. He was so amazed how wet she got. Never in all his years of fucking, had he met a woman whose pussy was as wet and sweet as Cheryl's. It drove him crazy. Cheryl told him he brought it out of her. She had been wet like that for Chuck but not as much as she was when she was with Morris.

"Baby, are you still there?" Morris said to Cheryl.

She was so wrapped up in her thoughts of their lovemaking that she hadn't even heard him still talking to her. "Oh, my bad. Yes, I'm still here. So what's up, boo? I was daydreaming about how we really make a mess," Cheryl told him and then giggled.

"Well, you don't have to daydream. Come get this dick. I miss that sweet, juicy pussy," Morris told her and grabbed his instantly hardened dick. He was always aroused and ready for Cheryl. When they were together, he felt like a teenager all over again. Each moment spent with Cheryl was amazing. He knew it wasn't right or fair to either of their spouses, but shit, he couldn't help it. Neither one of them could help it; they were too gone.

"Damn, baby. This pussy sure does miss daddy's dick, but I have to get home. I'm just wrapping up dinner and drinks with Joy, and I told Chuck I would be home soon. Sorry, daddy, not tonight." Cheryl hated to tell him no, but she had to have some self-control. They needed to be really careful, or their little secret would not be a secret anymore.

But Morris wasn't trying to hear that, and he wasn't taking "no" for an answer. He had to be home too, and he knew the risk he would be taking, but he was willing to take that risk. "No baby, don't do daddy like that. I thought you missed us," Morris pleaded with her trying, to sound so sad, so she could give in. It had always worked, except once, and Morris was sure it was going to work this time.

"I can't, and of course I miss y'all. Damn, I would love to taste you right now, but, baby the timing is crazy. I promise we will make it up to both of you." She didn't want to leave him on ice like that—him or his good-ass dick, but she had to. Besides, what if Chuck wanted some tonight? She couldn't keep telling him no.

Morris really wasn't trying to hear that shit, and he really wasn't taking "no" for an answer. "Listen, baby, I understand, but I miss you, and I'm going crazy. I tell you what: Meet me by that warehouse down from your house, so I could see you and taste that pussy. Then you won't be too far from home," he told her. He was serious as a heart attack.

Cheryl couldn't do anything but laugh at his determination. He was dead-ass. He seemed to amuse her with what came out his mouth and the crazy shit he thought of. He was so spontaneous, and it made her want him even more. She stayed silent, trying to think of a comeback with to tell him no, but she wasn't quick enough.

"No need to get silent trying to come up with some shit. You know this is a good plan. So just meet me there, baby," Morris told her.

"Man, what if we get caught, Morris?" Cheryl asked him.

"That's the best part about it, knowing there's that possibility of somebody seeing me beating and sucking on that good-ass pussy. I know for a fact we won't get caught, so stop playing. We're wasting time, baby," Morris said to her as he cruised through traffic to meet her.

Cheryl shook her head, she couldn't do anything but laugh and agree to meet him. The excitement in his voice was the adrenaline she needed. So they meet at the warehouse. When Cheryl got there, Morris was there waiting by the back of his truck with his dick out and at attention. Cheryl loved the view she was seeing, so without saying a word she walked over to him, grabbed his dick, and went to work.

Morris was moaning uncontrollably as Cheryl sucked and licked on his dick, teasing him. Then slowly she went all the way down, letting his dick touch the back of her throat. She took it so deep her nose touched his stomach. Morris went crazy. It felt so damn good how deep she took his dick in. Cheryl was moaning and sucking him up really good.

"That's right, baby. Suck this dick. Wet daddy's dick up, baby," Morris said to her. Cheryl made sure she granted his wish; she wet his dick up really good. She continued to suck him long and slow and deep. After a few more licks, slurps, and kisses on his dick, Morris released all in Cheryl's mouth, and she swallowed every bit of what he let out. She continued to suck the head of his dick, causing the tingling and funny sensation to flow throw his body. Morris couldn't take it. He tried so hard to get away. He was moving and scramming around. That always made Cheryl laugh and feel good at the same time because she knew she had done her thing. She loved to tease him; it made her wetter.

"Why are you running? You can take it," Cheryl teased him as she finally released his manhood from her mouth. She looked up at him, licked her lips, and smiled. He pulled her up closer and hugged her, grabbing on her nice, round, pillow-soft ass.

"Baby, you gon' let daddy get some of that juicy pussy?" he whispered in her ear. To feel the vibration in his voice and smell that sexy smell of his Armani cologne made her melt. That pussy was really throbbing.

She smiled and whispered back at him, "Yes, daddy, come get this pussy." Morris picked her up, placed part of her body in the back of the truck, and bent her over. Her ass was up in the air, just the way both of them liked it. Her pussy was peeking out at him, and it was oh so wet. Morris began to taste her juices as they flowed, and he licked and sucked on her clit from the back. He had his left hand placed on her back, making sure she was bent over and arched perfectly. Cheryl was moaning as she enjoyed the pleasure he was giving her in between licks and sucks.

Morris told her, "Cum, baby. I want to taste it, baby. Cum all over my tongue."

Cheryl felt like she was on a cloud; that moment was perfect. She could feel the breeze from the night air, which made it even better. Her pussy started throbbing and jumping faster and her moans got louder. She was cumming. Morris cold feel the warm, sweet sensation of her juices as they squirted out of her pussy. He was eating like it was his last meal.

"Damn, baby, you taste so good. Are you ready for your dick?" he asked her. Without letting her answer, he stood up completely and slowly entered his hardened dick inside of her. "Shit, baby, this pussy feels so good," Morris said to Cheryl as he looked down at her ass and watched how he slowly pushed his dick in and out of her. Each time he entered, she tightened her pussy and gripped that dick. That drove him crazy, and the both of them were in sexual bliss, enjoying the feeling. They were zoned out and had forgotten they were in public.

"Baby, yes, get this pussy. Morris, beat this pussy, baby, beat it. Oh my god, I love this dick, baby. Yes, right there. Stroke this pussy. Oh, my!" Cheryl was ranting and moaning. It felt so good that she couldn't help but shout it out.

All Morris could say was, "Damn." He went in and out, and he bit down on his lip. "Shit, this pussy is so wet. Damn, I want you to cum all over this dick, baby. Cum on daddy's dick, baby. Cum all over this dick, baby."

"I'm cumming, Morris. Oh shit, I'm cumming, baby."

"Damn, I love this pussy. Yes, baby, I feel it. Do you feel it, baby?"

"Yes, I feel it, daddy! Damn."

They both had reached their climax, and he fell on top of her as she fell flat on her stomach once they both came. They laid there for a few moments longer and then got up. Cheryl always carried wipes with her, so they both got cleaned up. They chatted a bit and then left.

The whole drive home, Cheryl was smiling. She felt so good. She checked her phone to see if Chuck had called. He hadn't, so she decided to call him. The phone went straight to voicemail, so she called back, and the same thing happened. She figured maybe his phone was dead, so she called the house phone, but it just kept ringing. She hung up and figured maybe he was sleep. She stopped at the gas station by the house to get a drink. As she pulled in, she noticed Chuck's truck parked by the door of the gas station. She wanted to go say something, but instead she pulled in the cut to see when he came out. He came out, got in his truck, and pulled off. He was going in the opposite direction of the house. She didn't want to, but she started following him. She kept her distance and was surprised he hadn't noticed he was being followed. As she continued, she noticed she was going mighty far. *Where in the hell could he be going?* she thought to herself. Finally, he stopped at a motel hidden off in the cut. She turned her engine off and waited nervously to see who he was about to meet. Her heart was racing. True enough, she had just finished being with Morris… But shit, she would've never even thought to be with Morris had this trifling bitch not been out doing what the fuck he was doing.

A few seconds later, the car pulled up, and look whose car it was! "You have to be kidding me. These two bitches are really trying me," Cheryl said to herself. She was about to get out the car with her gun and fuck both of them up, but then she paused as she saw the body exit the car. Tears came from out of nowhere and ran down Cheryl's face. She couldn't believe her eyes. She was so hurt. She was screaming, but no sound was coming out. "What the fuck, why in the fuck?" she yelled. Her body was stiff, and she couldn't move. Cheryl sat there the whole time crying. Time had gone by, and they had even left, and she was still sitting in the car. Her phone rang over a million times, but the sound of the rings sounded far away. Another hour later, Cheryl pulled herself together and made her way home.

Chapter Fourteen

WHEN SHE ARRIVED HOME, CHUCK was there. Before she could get out of the car, he came storming out the door in a panic, like he had been there all night waiting for her. "Cher, where the hell have you been? And why didn't you answer my calls? You got me worried and shit. Are you…"

Before another word could come out of his mouth, she slapped him so hard he forgot what he was going to say. "Cut that fuck shit out, pussy nigga," Cheryl said to him. She knew he hated those words, but she didn't give a fuck. By the look on his face, she could tell he was getting angry, and she was ready. "Yeah, you look shocked I said that, but guess what, pussy nigga. I don't give a flying fuck. I can't believe your raggedy ass. Then you got the nerve to pretend you've been here all night waiting on me. So you were waiting on me, Chuck? Huh. Were you, bitch?" Cheryl yelled at him and started walking towards the door.

Now he was scared. *Shit,* he thought to himself. He didn't know what to do or say at this point. He followed her in the house, where she was pacing back and forth in the kitchen. She didn't know how to deal with this. To think it was her profession!

"Lord, what to do?" she said. Chuck stood by the kitchen door and told her to calm down. He said they should sit and talk.

"Sit and talk? Really, do you actually think I want to talk to you right now? Honestly?" she asked him. Part of her wanted to reveal what she knew, but she had a better plan in mind. She was going to keep it to herself until the time was right. In the meantime, she planned on leaving the house for a while to map everything out. She never liked to make decisions when she was angry, so she decided to leave.

"Listen and listen good. I'm leaving, and please don't try and stop me. I will be out of this house for a while. Don't fucking call me or anything for shit," she told him. Then she headed towards the room to pack some bags.

"Are you fucking kidding me? Look, I understand you're pissed off, but we just need to talk about this. Remember, we have children, a family," he said to her, trying to plead with her.

"Nigga, you weren't thinking about all that when you were doing what the fuck you were doing," Cheryl replied to him. He stood there silently with a dumb a look on his face. "My point exactly. You didn't think, so don't think now. We will have a time to talk about all this shit—trust and believe that. But as for now, I suggest you leave me the fuck alone," Cheryl said, and she continued to pack. When she finally finished, she headed for the door.

Chuck wanted so badly to stand in her way, but he decided to let her cool. He figured she hadn't seen much because she didn't say much, but then again she was secretive and always waited and plotted how to reveal shit. He just watched her walk to the door. Once she got closer, tears fell down her face.

She couldn't believe her marriage was over. How could this be? Never in a million years would she have imagined saying these words. She turned and looked at Chuck. "By the way, make sure you get yourself a good attorney. I want a fucking divorce," Cheryl told him. Then she walked out the door.

The sound of those words were like a bullet going through Chuck's heart. He couldn't believe his ears. He stood there in the middle of the floor, and tears fell from his eyes. He was losing the love of his life, his family. How could this be?

A few weeks passed by, and Chuck still hadn't heard from Cheryl much. The only time they saw each other was when he came to see the kids, and even then she treated him like an invisible ghost. The kids wondered what was wrong with mommy and daddy, but they kept them out of the beef. Chuck constantly tried to think of ways he could get her back, but nothing worked. He sent flowers, jewelry, money, food, everything. He even hired someone to go to her office and sing their favorite song. Yeah, she may have smiled, but that didn't work at all. She still ignored him. Chuck was about to lose his mind. The thought of a divorce had never crossed his mind. He knew he had done some really grimy shit to her, but he wanted to fix it. Chuck went to visit a good friend of his to seek some guidance. When he got there, he decided not to bring it up. He realized that no one knew who his secret lover was, so he couldn't go through with it. "Shit," he said to himself and hit the steering wheel. He laid his head back on his head rest. Just as he closed his eyes, his cell rang.

He hurried to get it out of his pocket in hopes that it was Cheryl, but to his surprise it wasn't. It was the motherfucker who was causing him to lose everything. Chuck had been ignoring the calls for a few days, but this time he decided to answer. "What the fuck do you keep calling me for?" Chuck yelled through the phone. He was clearly pissed off, and his tone of voice told it all.

"Who the fuck do you think you're talking to like that? Remember, I could ruin your whole fucking life, so you better chill the fuck out," the person on the other end of the phone told Chuck. Chuck took a deep breath. He tried to keep his cool. He was already pissed off, and shit was already fucked up.

"Look, my peeps, now I don't know how much she knows, but she's asking me for a fucking divorce. So all that you're talking doesn't mean much to me," Chuck said. The phone was silent for a few moments, and then Chuck decided to end the call. With no warning or anything, he just hung up. He didn't have time for the bullshit. He had already fucked up really badly. He sat in his car for another hour or so before he decided to start driving. He finally drove himself home, which was the last place he wanted to be. The house he had once shared with his wife was no longer a home. He pulled in the garage and just sat in the car and cried. *God, what have I done?*

Tears flowed down his face like a running faucet. Never in all his years of living had he ever cried like this before. He felt it deep in his soul; he had lost, and there was no getting it back. *What the fuck was I thinking? How could I be so fucking stupid to even try this? Damn, I never wanted to lose my family.*

Chuck pulled out his cell phone and called his mom. She always helped ease his mind. "Hey, Chuckie! To what do I owe the pleasure of this call?" the sweet voice on the other end answered. Hearing her voice eased his pain just a tiny bit.

"Hey, Ma!" Chuck said in a dry tone. By the sound of his voice, she knew something was wrong. Chuck and his mom didn't talk often, but they had a great relationship. He knew she would be pissed off hearing what she had to say. She had always loved Chuck and Cheryl's relationship and always made him promise that he would do everything in his power to keep his wife and kids happy. Now he was calling her to tell her he had failed.

"What's the matter, boy? You sound like you lost your best friend," his mom replied to him. Chuck took a deep breath and let it out.

"I did lose my best friend, Ma. I fucked up. I fucked up bad, Ma!" Chuck told her. Tears slowly ran down his face as he told her. His mom was speechless, and she knew he was talking about Cheryl, but she hoped like hell he wasn't.

"Chuck, please tell me you're not talking about Cheryl," she told him.

"I'm sorry, Ma! I really am. I don't know what's wrong with me," he told her. Chuck decided to explain and tell his mom the secret that was causing him to get a divorce. She was pissed off at him. She was so mad that she told him a few words and hung up. He didn't even bother to call her back. He knew she was pissed, so he gave her time to cool off. He dreaded going into the house.

It was no longer a home because Cheryl wasn't there. After about an hour, he went inside the house.

He headed to the room, and he could tell that she had been there. He could smell the scent of her perfume. Chuck looked around the room to see if he could figure out what she had taken. After standing in a daze for a few minutes, Chuck lay down on the bed, buried his face in the pillow, and fell asleep. The next morning, Chuck was awakened by the sound of his kids. For a minute he thought he was dreaming until they jumped on top of him. He was so happy to see them and was even happier knowing that Cheryl was there. He didn't know what to expect seeing her. He played with them for a few minutes. He had missed them so much. Although he saw them all the time, it still wasn't the same.

A few minutes later, Cheryl came in the room. She looked over at them and forced a smile, but you could see the pain in her eyes. She looked away and headed to the closet to grab some more things. Chuck told the kids to go in their room for a few minutes. "Let daddy talk to mommy," Chuck told them. As soon as they ran out of the room, Cheryl turned around and rolled her eyes at him.

"Why did you tell them to leave? We have nothing to discuss," she said and continued to go through her things. Chuck took a deep breath and closed his eyes. He knew she would act this way, but it was worth trying.

"Cher, I know you're upset, but just hear me out, please," he begged her. Cheryl didn't want to talk to him at all, but she didn't want to start all that drama in front of the kids. So she held her anger and hoped he didn't piss her off.

"Go ahead, Chuck, but please don't think that anything you say is going to change my mind."

That just killed Chuck, but he went for it anyways. "Listen, I can understand your anger, and I don't blame you, but we've been together too long to let this tear us apart. I promise I will do whatever it takes to fix this. Divorce is not the solution," he told her. He looked to see her reaction, and by the way she turned around, he knew what was coming out of her mouth next wouldn't be nice.

"Do you hear yourself? Are you fucking serious? See, this is why I didn't want to talk to you. Chuck, there is no coming back from this. You're really thinking we can get past this? Seriously, Chuck?" Cheryl asked him.

Chuck just stood there and looked at her. He knew part of what she was saying was right, but he didn't want it to be. "This is crazy, Cher. We can at least try therapy or something. I mean, you do this for a living. Do you tell all your clients to go straight to divorce?" He should have never said that.

"Before I snap on your stupid ass, I'm going to leave. I swear you are so fucking stupid. What the fuck would have made you say that stupid shit? Man, Chuck, I really don't have time for this shit right now. I only came to get a few things. I didn't even expect you to be here. Now is not the time to talk cause you're going to make me go the fuck off. So you want me to leave the kids with you, or what are you gon' do?" Cheryl looked at Chuck with a stern look in her face.

Everything in her wanted to punch him in his shit. Just being in the same room with him made her sick to her stomach.

Chuck was just standing there looking like a puppy. Cheryl was getting impatient with him just standing there looking at her, so she reached for her bags and headed for the door. Chuck grabbed her arm, and she yanked her arm away from him.

"Cheryl, don't do this. Can you at least say you will think about it?" Chuck begged her.

"Don't do this! Chuck, did you think when you were doing it? Damn, and you brought it so close to home. What the fuck were you thinking? Someone that close, you sick, stupid motherfucker? Kiss my ass!" Cheryl told him. She walked out of the room, and you could see smoke coming from her head; that's how mad she was. She was pissed off.

She went into the kids' room, gave them a kiss, and told them she would see them later. Chuck had walked to their room and watched Cheryl hug them from the doorway. It burned his soul that he was about to lose all this over some bullshit. Cheryl walked past him, and for the sake of the kids, she told him bye. Chuck said, "Bye," and watched her leave.

Cheryl got to her car and broke down in tears. Divorce or separating her family had never entered into her mind until now. She knew she was having an affair, too, but Chuck brought it to this point. Plus, he was fucking someone they knew, and fuck, the person it was made it even worse! "I can't believe this pussy ass nigga tried me like this. Why in the hell did this have to happen to me?" Cheryl yelled and screamed to herself in the car. She knew her marriage wasn't exempt from shit like this, but damn, she thought she was prepared if it ever happened. She wished like hell it was a bad dream and she would wake up soon, but it was her reality. She had no clue what to do. She sat in the car for a few more minutes, fixed her face, pulled out of the driveway, and headed to the office.

Chapter Fifteen

CHERYL FINALLY REACHED THE OFFICE. "Hey, boss lady. How are you today?" her assistant greeted her as she came through the door.

"Hello there! I'm well, and you?" Cheryl replied.

"Great. Your appointment isn't until another two hours. I didn't expect you this early," she told Cheryl as she looked at the calendar.

"I know, but I have some online sessions and a lot of other things to do, Miss Thing."

"Oh yeah, you are right. Excuse me, boss lady," her assistant said, teasing her.

Cheryl smiled and asked her, "Do I have any messages?"

"Yes, here you are. Do you want me to grab you anything?" she asked Cheryl. Cheryl didn't hear her because she was too busy going through the messages. When she saw one was from Sam, she froze in place. All the rage and anger she had held inside was coming out, and she almost exploded. She had to catch herself and remember where she was. She crumbled up the paper with Sam's name on it. She snapped out of her daze when her assistant kept calling her name.

"Earth to Cher."

"Oh, my bad. What were you saying?" Cheryl asked her.

She chuckled and said, "I was asking if you wanted me to get you anything."

"Oh, no, I'm good. Thanks. Just let me know when my appointment gets here, and hold all my calls unless it's an emergency," Cheryl told her.

"Sure thing, boss lady."

Cheryl headed to her office. When she got in her office, she sat at her desk and tried to clear her head and get ready for her clients. She needed to focus, but being that she dealt with relationship issues for a living made it worse. Yeah, they say to separate your work life from your personal life, but how could she when now her personal life was exactly like her work life? This shit drove her crazy, but she was good at hiding her pain, and that's exactly what she did. Cheryl looked down at the time and noticed it was time for her virtual conversation. She grabbed her note pad and turned on the computer. Her appointment was a little early, and her instant message notification went off.

Ping

SoInLove41: *Hello, the beautiful Cheryl.*

Cheryl: *Hello, Mr. SoInLove41. How are you today?*

SoInLove41: *So-so, but I'm making it.* ☺

Cheryl: *Well, let's see if we can change that so-so. So what's going on?*

SoInLove41: *The boo and I are not clicking, and she's having some financial trouble, which that means I will have to invest most of my money and time to her.*

Cheryl: *You sound like you don't want to help her. Don't tell me you're on the brink of giving up.*

SoInLove41: *I don't mind helping her. It's just tough, and everything always ends up falling on me. Her kids and all that.*

Cheryl: *Hmm. That sounds tough. You sound like you're not really up for it.*

SoInLove41 *To be honest, not really. I always feel like everything is always about her.*

Cheryl: *Well dang, since the last time we talked, you sound fed up.*

SoInLove41: ☹☹

Cheryl: *Let me ask you, have you told her that you feel like everything is about her?*

SoInLove41 *Yep, and she turns it around and snaps.*

Cheryl: *Maybe it just seems that way to you because you are able to do more than she can. Have you ever thought of it that way?*

SoInLove41 *Damn, this is why I love talking to you. You are so right*

Cheryl *You're funny. But really, I feel she wants to do as much for you as you do for her, but there are limits to what she can do at the moment. But you truly have to follow your heart. I don't know her well, but from what you've told me, she is a keeper. She just needs a little work*

SoInLove41: *A lot of work (LOL)! I just hope it's worth it in the end, and you know money changes people.*

Cheryl: Not really. People let that interfere, but if you truly love someone, you would be with them if they were broke or rich. What matters most is loyalty, love, and respect.

SoInLove41: True that, but how do you know if the person really loves you for you and not for what you have or can do?

Cheryl: Good question, but the answer is in your heart sometimes. I feel that way because if you truly and deeply feel that that's all the person is in it for, then that's exactly what it is. The signs are usually right in our faces. Does she give you any reason to feel that way?

Cheryl's phone began to ring. She looked down and saw it was Chuck. She didn't want to answer, but the kids were with him. She didn't want to stop her session, so she answered quickly. "What's up? Are the kids okay?" she asked.

"Yeah. I'm just letting you know we will be at my mom's," Chuck told her. That kind of pissed her off. She knew how strongly his mother felt about their marriage, and Chuck was trying to pull a fast one. But she didn't even have time to argue with him.

"Okay. Bye, Chuck" she said. Then she hung up and finished her session.

SoInLove41: No, but at times I think of what my ex-wife did, and I guess I listen to what people say.

Cheryl: You are going to have to let what happened to you in the past go. If you really want a different future, you can't read a book backwards to get to the next chapter ahead.

SoInLove41: *You're right, but it's scary.*

Cheryl: *And it's okay to listen to people sometimes, but at the end of the day, like I always say, whatever choice you make, it's for you and no one else.*

SoInLove41: *But my ex-wife and I connected in ways I can't explain.*

Cheryl: *I feel you, but you have to realize she is not your ex-wife.*

SoInLove41 *My ex-wife was very thoughtful, and we never went through things like me and my new girl do.*

Cheryl *You may still be in love with the image of your ex-wife, and you're trying to mimic that in this relationship. Let me tell you, that is only going to make it worse.*

SoInLove41 *True! Damn, you are so wise*

Cheryl: *Everyone is not the same; you have to remember that. And I know you may miss those things with your ex-wife, but you have to give this relationship a fair chance.*

SoInLove41: ☺ ☺ *Thanks. You are truly good at what you do. You really know it all.*

Cheryl: *No, I don't know it all.* ☺ *But give it a fair shot.*

SoInLove41: *Okay, I will. You have a good day.*

Cheryl: *You too.*

Cheryl logged off and answered a few e-mails, and then she met with her client. After her meeting, she gathered her things and called it a day. On her way out, Nadine called. She had been calling all day, so she decided to answer her this time.

"Hi, Nadine," Cheryl greeted her.

"Hey, Cheryl. I'm so sorry to keep bugging you, but I'm about to go crazy," Nadine said to her.

"It's okay. I'm free now for a few minutes. What's up?"

"It's official; he is cheating. The other night he came home smelling like a bitch's perfume. I know I normally jump the gun, but I'm so sure now," Nadine said. You could hear in her voice that she had been crying.

Cheryl sat down on the couch because she knew this was going to be a long call. "How sure are you? Maybe he met with a client." Cheryl tried to reason with her, but Nadine was sure of it this time.

"Cheryl, I hear you. I know I had no right going through his things, but I found hotel receipts to hotels he's been going to when his punk ass was supposed to be at his office. I even found a receipt where he bought this bitch some pink roses and a fucking watch. He bought this bitch a watch. How could he?" Nadine started yelling and crying.

Cheryl felt her pain through the phone, and it made her think about her problems with Chuck. *Damn what the fuck is wrong with these men?* she thought. She really didn't know what to say to Nadine to ease the pain. It was tough.

"Oh wow, Nadine! I'm sorry, sweetie. I can truly understand what you're feeling right now."

"Cheryl, I gave him my all, and he doesn't appreciate me. Do you know he's been seeing this bitch on every business trip he goes on? This shit is getting out of hand. He is starting to like her emotionally, and that's what hurts the most," Nadine said through her tears.

"How do you know it's emotionally?" Cheryl asked although that was a dumb question. If he brought this bitch a watch, he had to be feeling her in some type of way.

"I could tell. I feel it. Wow, this shit is killing me. I want to fuck him up so bad. I should poison that bitch tonight," Nadine said.

"No! Don't do that. First you have to calm down. I know it's hard, but you don't want to make any decisions out of anger. I know that it's easier said than done, but you don't want to do something that could ruin you in the process of trying to get back at him. If you like, we could meet now, so we could talk about this more," Cheryl told her. She didn't want her to do something that could potentially cause her to be in a bad situation. She understood her pain, but for every action, there was a reaction. Nadine wasn't really in the mood to see Cheryl; she just wanted to talk to her.

"No, that's fine. I just needed someone to talk to. I really just need some time to myself to think on how I'm going to approach this. I really want to catch him and the bitch together, so I can fuck the both of them up," Nadine said to Cheryl. Everything in her wanted to fuck him up, but she was going to get his ass. She was going to start following him and even put a tracking device on his car and phone. She didn't tell Cheryl her plans because she knew Cheryl would try and talk her out of it. "Naw, really it's cool. You're right. I need to chill before I do something I will regret. So I'mma relax. Maybe I'll go to my sister's house for a few days to cool off," Nadine told Cheryl.

"Okay cool! You know I'm just a phone call away if you need me."

"Thanks a lot. I really appreciate you, Cheryl. I'm so glad to have met you," Nadine told Cheryl. They said their goodbyes and hung up. Cheryl finally left the office to head to Chuck's mom's house to get the kids. The whole drive over there, she was trying to keep herself calm. *I can't believe this nigga has me going way over here, knowing damn well I said I don't want to talk,* Cheryl thought to herself as she got closer to Chuck mom's house. When she reached the driveway she sat in the car to gather herself. Cheryl put her head down on the steering wheel for a few moments. Then she heard the kids voice playing outside, and Cheryl got out the car and walked in the house.

Chapter Sixteen

IT HAD BEEN A WHILE since Joy and John talked. They hadn't spoken since the last time they saw each other and John flipped out. Neither of them called each other, but Joy was missing him like crazy. Joy had a lot of pride, and she never wanted to be the one to give in first, but she couldn't help it. She was missing him, so she called him. She was so nervous and didn't even expect him to answer.

"Well, well, I guess you finally made up your mind," John said as he answered the phone. Joy sucked her teeth. That really pissed her off. She wanted to hang up on his dumb ass. Now she wished like hell she had stuck to what she always did and let a motherfucker call her first.

"Wow, are you serious? You can't even say 'hi' first?" she replied to John with an annoyed tone in her voice.

He let out a chuckle and said, "Hi, Joy. How are you? Is that better?"

Joy laughed at his stupidity. "You are real funny. I'm good, John, so what's up with you? Do you still have your ass on your shoulders?" she barked back at him. She figured since he wanted to be stupid and slick, she would do the same, but John didn't like that response.

"Really? You must still want to play games. So let's cut the small talk. You had more than enough time to think things over. So what have you come up with, my dear?" John bluntly said to her.

Now Joy was really pissed. She knew where he was coming from, but damn. "Look, we haven't talked in a few weeks. Damn, you don't even know if I'm okay or what I'm going through. You just want to start this bullshit up again. You really think it's so fucking simple."

John didn't even let Joy finish. "Man, go on with all that bullshit. Remember, your child's father is my brother, so if something was wrong with your trust, I would've known. I know everything, so miss me with that shit. So obviously you still want to play with my feelings and fucking emotions, right?" John asked her.

Joy took the phone from her ear and looked at it in shock. She was about sick of this shit with him. She loved him, but fuck, if she had to constantly go through this bullshit, was it really worth it? Although he had a point: If they loved each other, why did it have to be a secret? But shit, this was one secret that was safer in the dark, at least for now. John didn't understand that at all.

"John, you're really starting to piss me off with this shit. See, you don't have shit to lose. That's why you don't give a fuck. I love you, I do, and I hate to keep creeping and sneaking around just as much as you do. But there's a lot at stake. I could possibly lose my child, and you know your brother would have a field day with this. You have to understand me, baby," Joy told John, trying to reason with him and see if he would understand her, but he still wasn't trying to hear it. John was fed up.

"You know what, Joy, you're right. I don't have shit to lose. My fear this whole time was losing you, but fuck it and fuck you. See, you wanna talk about secrets getting out and how you love me. Bitch do you even know what love is?" John snapped. Joy was on the other end shocked. She couldn't say a word. He continued, "Close your mouth. Yes, I said it. Bitch, you pretend to be a victim. See, my stupid ass fell in love with you cause I saw you were a good woman, and my brother didn't appreciate you. Now here I am, trying to be that king you deserve, but I'm done. Enough is enough. We've been creeping for over a year. How much more time do you need, baby?" John told her. You could hear the anger in his tone. Joy really didn't know how to respond. He was really pissed. She cared, but part of her needed to think about what was best for her.

"I can't believe you, you stupid fucker. If that's how you feel, oh fucking well. I told you when the time was right the shit would be done, but you can't get that part. Maybe you're right. Fuck it all, fuck you, and fuck your so-called feelings all that bullshit. I guess we have come to a fucking conclusion, and I got your, bitch pussy nigga. I'm not going to take disrespect at all. So if this is how you want it to end, then let it be," Joy snapped back at him. She was pissed. She never wanted to end things, and especially not on a bad note, but fuck it.

John started laughing an evil laugh. "Okay, baby girl, you won. I'm glad you like playing with people's feelings, so I guess this is the end of us. But you fucked over the wrong person.

See, this secret can still be revealed with or without your sneaky, trifling ass."

"Trifling? Fuck, nigga, who are you calling trifling? Kiss my ass, John. I was nothing but good to you, and this is how you repay me. Cool. Go ahead. You want to try me and air shit out? We will see who gets the last laugh," Joy threatened him.

John found that even funnier. "Really, you were so good to me? But just a few months ago, you were still fucking my brother again. And you fucked him the same night me and you fucked." Joy couldn't breathe. When she heard him say that, she had no come back. "Hello, are you there?" John said sarcastically. "You thought I wouldn't find out, but like a fool I stuck around. And, sweetheart, that's just one of your many secrets. You fucked over the wrong dude. I'mma let you go, but I will leave you with this. Ain't no secret safe in the dark!" John told her then hung up. He was pissed, and she really had fucked up because now she was the enemy.

Joy sat there with the phone in her hand in shock. The words he said to her replayed over and over in her head. She was scared as hell now. She knew one day it would have to be revealed but not like this. She knew now she had to come up with a plan to fix this. Joy knew now she would have to tell Cheryl about this secret love affair.

Chapter Seventeen

"Mommy, Mommy!" The kids ran up to Cheryl, giving her a big hug. She held them and squeezed them tight.

"Hello there, baby girl," said the voice of the sweetest lady ever.

"Hi, Momma J," she replied. She went to give Chuck's mom a hug. She hadn't seen her in a while, but when she did it was always pleasant. Momma J always told Chuck, "Son, I'm so proud of you. You have finally found your soulmate. Don't ever let her get away." Momma J and Chuck's dad had been married for what seemed like forever, and when he passed away, Momma J had never remarried. She always said you only get one true love, one soulmate, and her husband was hers. She really valued marriage and family, and she always tried to instill that faith and belief in her kids, especially Chuck. So when he told her he had had an affair, it burned her soul. She knew Cheryl had every right to be angry, but she really wanted them to try and get past this. Cheryl could sense the conversation coming up, and only for the sake of Momma J she would be willing to talk. But her mind was made up, so it really wouldn't make a difference. She just wanted all this to be over with already.

"So how have you been, Momma J?"

"I've been okay up until now when Chuckie came calling me with this nonsense about divorce," Momma J replied.

Cheryl let out a long sigh because this was going to be one ugly conversation. She looked at the kids and told them to go play. Then she turned back to Momma J. "Yes, Momma J, I feel the same way you feel, and it's messed up it has come to this point. But I guess that's life, and things happen," Cheryl replied to her nonchalantly.

Momma J didn't like Cheryl's response, but she couldn't knock her feeling. "I hear you. Although you sound like therapist-Cheryl instead of human-being-Cheryl. You and Chuck know how I feel about y'all's relationship," she told Cheryl.

"I know, and believe me as much as you value our marriage, I do, too. But there is only so much a person can take, and this is a human being speaking. I love Chuck with all my heart, and I would have never thought of ending our marriage. But see, he didn't value this marriage," Cheryl said while fighting back tears. She was determined not to cry. Momma J motioned for her to sit on the couch, and Chuck walked in the room looking like a lost puppy.

"Sit your ass down, Chuck!" Momma J ordered him. Chuck sat down, and then the room got silent for a few moments. There was so much tension, you could cut it with a knife. Momma J hated that.

"Look, we have to find a way to fix this. Cheryl, you're always giving advice and helping others. Now it's time for you to listen and get some help," Momma J told Cheryl. She really had no clue how bad this shit was. Cheryl didn't want to be rude or anything, but this was a waste.

"Momma J, no offense, but it's no use. Really, it's done."

Momma J sucked her teeth. She was getting pissed with Cheryl. Chuck was a bit annoyed, too. "Ma, I told you she wouldn't listen. She doesn't care. I know I fucked up. I get that, but I'm sorry. I want to make it right, but it takes the both of us to do that," Chuck said, pleading his case.

Cheryl looked at him like she wanted to chop his ass up. "Well, the both of us didn't have a fucking affair, now did we?" Cheryl lashed back at him, and then she got up to leave. Momma J grabbed her arm to stop her.

"Cheryl, baby, don't go," she told Cheryl.

"Momma J, really, it's not going to work. I don't want it to end, but there is no coming back from this. And it's been going on for a while," Cheryl told Momma J.

Momma J looked at Chuck with fire in her eyes. "Chuck, is this true? You called and told me it was a one-time thing. So you lied to me?" She was now pissed off with him. He sat in the chair not wanting to say a word, but he felt backed up in a corner. Both Cheryl and Momma J were just staring at him, waiting for him to say something, but he just sat there fidgeting with his fingers looking like a damn fool.

Cheryl was getting agitated. "Man, forget all of this. Enough is enough. Momma J, I'm leaving." Cheryl started walking towards the door. Chuck got up and went behind her.

"Cheryl, I told you I was sorry. I understand you're hurt, and I never meant to hurt you. Baby, you have to believe that. Please, we need to try and get past all this. I know it won't happen overnight, but…"

Cheryl didn't even let him finish. His voice was starting to annoy her, and she was trying not to snap. "Chuck, I'm trying not to disrespect you or your mom's house, but there is no hope for this. You tried me the first time, and I gave you a chance, Chuck, and you fucking tried me again. So what makes you think we have a chance?" Cheryl said to him.

Chuck looked at her crazily. "Cheryl, you haven't even made this easy for me lately. Shit, you're always angry, and you bring your work home. I know that's no excuse, but I'm sorry…"

"Chuck, what the fuck? Do you hear yourself? You sound so fucking stupid right now. All that you're talking about is irrelevant, Chuck. Now get out my way, and leave me alone," she told him as she tried to continue to leave. Chuck was so pissed, so now he was ready to snap.

"Fuck, Cheryl! You really want it to end. It's obvious you didn't want to be in it. I'm trying, and I stuck by you when you pulled that bullshit that you pulled back then. Now you want to come talking all this shit around Momma J like you're fucking perfect. You know I love you, and our family means the world to me," Chuck went off, but if he only knew he had fucked up… Now things were really about to get heated, especially since Momma J had come into the room where they were and tried to calm them down.

"Wait a minute. I won't allow both of you to stand here and disrespect each other like this. It's obvious you both have had secrets or things you've done, and you've made it through it all.

Cheryl, you really mean to tell me you can't get past this over time? You two are a strong union, and I hate to see it torn apart."

Cheryl looked at Momma J with a stern look on her face. She couldn't believe what she was hearing. She knew Momma J meant well, but Cheryl felt the blame was being placed all on her, and she didn't like that one bit. She kept trying to leave, and they wouldn't let her, so now she was about to unleash all her anger. This was truly the end.

"So, Chuck, do you feel I need to get past this and try and make it work?" She looked at Chuck.

He was a bit confused by the question although he figured she was being sarcastic, and that made him mad. "Cheryl, you know that's how I feel, so why in the fuck would you ask me that stupid-ass question?" Chuck said to her.

Momma J was just standing there. But that's exactly what Cheryl wanted—for him to get slick. Cheryl started clapping and laughing hysterically. Momma J and Chuck looked at Cheryl, and then she stopped laughing.

"See, Momma J, I know how you feel, and trust me, I love your Chuckie, and this he knows. But unfortunately this marriage is ending," she said to them. Momma J was about to say something. "Wait, before each of you decide to say anything, let me finish," Cheryl told them as she held her hand up and motioned them to be quiet. Both Chuck and Momma J looked at each other. They had never seen Cheryl like this. Cheryl didn't give a fuck at this point how either of them felt.

"Like I was saying, it's over, and I mean it. There is no working anything out. Yeah, I know I give advice for a living. I have never encouraged anyone to leave unless it was beyond staying. And this bullshit is beyond that. See, not only is Mr. Chuck here having an affair, but he's having one with someone we know. Someone I've let in my home, someone who has played with our kids, someone I considered a friend."

Chuck's eyes got big. All this time, she knew his secret. He didn't know what to do to stop her.

"Yeah, you thought I didn't have a clue, huh, Mr. Chuck? Or should I say Mrs. Chuck?" Cheryl asked him. You could now see smoke coming from his head. Momma J was lost.

"What are you talking 'bout, Cheryl? Chuck, what is she talking about?" Momma J asked them both.

Chuck held his head down in shame. He couldn't believe his ears. Cheryl really knew more than he thought she knew. *WOW!* He thought to himself. His mom was still standing, asking, "What the hell is going on, Chuck?" but he was frozen. He couldn't reply. He was speaking, but his voice was weak.

Cheryl didn't give a fuck, and the fact that he was in a state of shock made it easier. "Well, since Chuck won't tell you, I will. There is no way in hell I will stay married to a man who likes to push another man's shit and get his shit pushed in!" Cheryl yelled.

Momma J's mouth dropped and she yelled, "No! Please tell me this is not so. Please, god, that's not what I'm hearing," Momma J cried

"Yes, it's so. You heard right. Chuck is fucking his best friend. All this time, I thought he was fucking Samantha, but he's been fucking her husband. Nasty, gay, pussy-ass nigga. I can't believe this punk-ass shit. I gave you my all, and this how I'm repaid," Cheryl said.

"I'm not fucking gay. This was never supposed to happen. I don't know…"

"You don't know what, Chuck? How the fuck are you not gay, but you're fucking your homeboy? Get the fuck out of here, nigga. You thought you could keep this shit quiet? Naw sweetie, you must have forgot. There ain't no secret safe in the dark."

Cheryl stormed out the door and left Chuck and Momma J standing there together. She put the kids in the car and left. She wanted to break down so badly, but she would not while they were in the car. She kept it together till she got to her mom's. When she got there, she let the kids inside. She was outside, and her phone rang. It was an unknown number. Normally she wouldn't answer, but something told her to.

"Hello," she answered.

"Hello, is this Cheryl Michaels?" the unknown caller asked.

"Yes, this is she. May I ask who is calling?"

"Hi, Cheryl. I'm Detective Lewis with the Miami-Dade Police Department," the male voice said.

When he said that, Cheryl's heart dropped. She sat on the bench and took a deep breath. "Hi, Detective. How can I help you?" Cheryl asked him.

"I'm sorry to have to deliver you such bad news. This isn't easy for me to have to do," he said and then he paused. He now had Cheryl nervous as hell, and tears started forming in her eyes.

"What are you talking about, sir? And how did you get my name and number?" she said in a somewhat agitated voice.

"You were listed as a next of kin for Keyshia Daniels. Like I said, this isn't easy, but I'm sorry to tell you Mrs. Daniels is dead."

An instant chill came over her body, and then tears ran down her face. This had to be a bad dream. "Please, sir, tell me you're lying or that this is a mistake. It has to be. Please, God, no. This isn't true."

Cheryl dropped the phone and broke down to her knees crying. She couldn't believe it. Her best friend, her sister… "No, please, God, this can't be true!" she yelled. Her mom heard her and came running outside to see what was wrong with her. She found Cheryl crying uncontrollably.

"Cher, baby, what's wrong?"

"Momma, why, why did this happen? I should've been there to do something. No, please, I can't take this," Cheryl cried. Her mom asked her again. "Momma, its Keyshia! She's dead!" Cheryl said and continued crying.

Her mom didn't know what to do. She knew how close they were, and Keyshia was like a daughter to her. Her eyes filled with tears, and she didn't know what to do. She ran and grabbed the phone and called Joy. She told Joy what happened, and she went crazy over the phone. An hour later, Joy was there to be with her sister, her friend. They sat and cried and consoled each other the rest of the night.

About the Author

SHARMEKA BALLARD WAS BORN JANUARY 20, 1986, in Miami, Florida. She was born and raised in the Liberty City area, where most people would call the projects or the ghetto. Ballard was raised by her mother and grandparents. Her father was not around. Growing up for Sharmeka was hard, and part of what she went through is the reason she began to write. She always knew she had a gift and was determined to become a successful writer. Sharmeka loved reading urban novels as a teenager, which inspired her even more to become a writer. She began writing in her early teenage years. Her success as a young writer led to her creation of *Soul of A Teenager,* which was published in 2009. *Soul of A Teenager* is a collection of poems about a journey through a teenager's life, filled with different emotions. She was recognized in many different publications. She continues her unending pursuit and commitment to furthering her opportunity in becoming a successful and aspiring writer.

CPSIA information can be obtained
at www.ICGtesting.com
Printed in the USA
LVOW11s1503200617
538749LV00001B/180/P